COSETTE

The Wilted Rose

Osvaldo (Waldo) Zappa

To my friend Neville
with best wishes
Waldo Zappa
April 8, 2014

Produced by:

FriesenPress

Suite 300 – 852 Fort Street

Victoria, BC, Canada V8W 1H8

www.friesenpress.com

Distributed to the trade by The Ingram Book Company

For Jacqueline,
to whom without this would merely be a story.
For Jacqueline,
to whom this is an epitaph and a love letter.
For Jacqueline,
whose trials and tribulations
are laid to rest in this book.

INTRODUCTION

The drama that unfolds on a daily basis in this story is the revelation of a dementia patient, whose behavior and actions are puzzling and often irrational, and the reaction of the caregiver, whose challenges and patience are at the core of caregiving. Dementia (Alzheimer's) is a disabling disease that affects mostly the elderly. The majority of people with Alzheimer's are over sixty-five. But Alzheimer's is not just a disease of old age. Up to five per cent of people with the disease have early onset in their forties or fifties.

In exploring the labyrinth of the disease, the writer chronicles a story of care and love for his wife, who is afflicted by dementia, as well as the painful personal experiences that have helped him cope with this gargantuan task. Preoccupied with the state of his wife's health by recording daily occurrences, he has often ignored his own health issues, which, if left unattended, risk his ability to play the effective role of caregiver. Paradoxically, writing about his wife's state of mind has had a therapeutic effect on his own personal turmoil.

It has been through a commitment to his wife's needs that the writer responded to the task of caring, and he now wishes to share with other caregivers, faced with similar situations, the bridge they have built for this painful journey of discovery and understanding. The general reading public may also learn from these pages more about this global mind destroyer, as experienced by the writer's wife. Readers will be transported into a strange world of sink holes, tricks of real and unreal truths that the mind often plays on the victims, and the responses by those tending to their wellbeing: the face-less caregivers.

This fictional memoir is the story of Cosette and her caregiver husband Marc, who writes short stories as a pastime. Their lives are topsy-turvy when Cosette is diagnosed with dementia, and her husband must care for her. However, through the turmoil surrounding his wife's illness, he too has been diagnosed with another disease—prostate cancer—that he must now conceal from his blind wife. For Cosette, there is only despair and, looking forward, there is nothing but darkness. Equally for Marc, there is the painful reality that he must continue to care for her in the silence of his own illness.

J.P.Sartre: *"It is therefore senseless to think of complaining since nothing has decided what we feel, what we live, or what we are.... Life begins on the other side of despair."*

However, there is also a part of the story that is told, a back story, happy/sad story that describes Cosette and her husband Marc, their courtship, marriage, and travels back to their countries of origin. This is where life together began for them.

"Home is where your story begins" reads a sign posted on her hospital bedroom wall when she became very ill. These are the souvenirs of two people in love, their pasts entwined.

En pensant aux souvenirs
nous nous rendons compte
d'avoir vecu. Effacer les
souvernirs c'est effacer la vie
Giovanni Costa, poet, (1940-2011)
Thinking of memories,
we realize we have
lived. To cancel
memories is to cancel life.

PART ONE

CHAPTER 1

When I stand in front of her to look into her lifeless eyes, my heart fills with pain. A frosty circle covers her right eye, a cataract resulting from a detached retina. The other eye looks nearly normal, but she is blind in both eyes. Her hands at times tremble, as an insidious tremor has affected her whole body. When she walks she reminds me of the turtle Aunt Alice has in her garden in France. When Cosette tries to stand up from a chair or a sofa, her balance is so unstable that I need to intervene to prevent her from falling backwards. To steady her, I place my hand on her back to guide her along. Even when using a cane, she is afraid of bumping against objects placed around the house. So I worry about her getting hurt.

But like a rose tossed by the merciless wind, she rocks, shedding petals before my eyes. Soon, only the stem will remain in my hand to remind me of its bloom.

As she rests on the sofa contemplating her surroundings, she tries to remember what the inside of the house used to look like when she could see. The reality is that things aren't always in the proper order, and space in her mind doesn't exist anymore. The house we have lived in for the past forty years has two storeys, with living quarters upstairs, and a family room, den, laundry room, and pantry with a large freezer located downstairs. As she comes down the stairs, running her hand along the wall, she still remembers the various large silkscreen reproduction of Canadian painters-one by A. Jackson, one of the Group of Seven (11). At the top of the stairs I placed a rope for her protection, and to the right is the kitchen, which connects with the dining room and the living room with sofas, side tables, and lamps. Angles and corners now confuse her.

The layout is an open plan, and so there are no doors separating these spaces on the east side of the house. Also upstairs in the living room is a glassed curio cabinet imported from Korea, made from cherry wood. In this curio are kept a number of items that she has forgotten still exist: two crystal vases, a silver coffee and tea server, and a silver ice bucket, all dating back to our tenth anniversary. It includes a *veritable porcelaine de France,* depicting Le Mont Saint Michel, while another one depicts various vignettes of *Le Vieux Quebec* (Old Quebec), and yes, a model of the ship Brilliance of the Seas—a must-have, the first cruise we took in the Caribbean—complete the menagerie. A large collage painted in 1971 by LiLian titled "City by night" hangs on one side of the cabinet. Two signed Inuit soapstone prints dating back to1985 hang from the other walls. A macrame art work made of knotted cord and depicting an owl that Cosette put together when she could see hangs on the wall near the front deck door. Completing the upstairs living quarters is a long corridor lined with several limited edition prints, which leads to the four bedrooms and the main bathroom.

For her, the art hanging on the walls are invisible reminders of the joy to watch and admire. Many pieces of furniture are scattered in the rooms that are now a labyrinth she must navigate to find her way about. Every day she sails into an unknown sea that denies her freedom and happiness, and my heart cries out into the darkness of her world. Our living room is now a minefield of bumps and obstacles.

"What's happening to me? I am blind, and now this; I just as well be dead!" She cries out. The outburst pierces my heart like an arrow. It is said that a heart must be broken to achieve strength, but where would the strength come from if not from the heart itself? But why would Cosette wish for her non-existence when there is more to life than the finality of it? I need to take a deeper look at the illness wrecking her mind and body—and with hers, mine also. To find out, I need to consult our family doctor.

*   *   *

Now I realize that nothing was ever ordinary with my wife Cosette. The visit with our family doctor is scheduled for September 2012; it might shed some light on what is worrying me about my wife.

In the late eighties, Cosette underwent surgery in one eye as a result of retinal detachment. Years later, after returning to work as a substitute French teacher and just before the Christmas holidays, she lost her one good eye. Statistically, the probability of losing both eyes because of retinal detachment is extremely rare. This circumstance dictated a readjustment to Cosette's way of life. Then, in the sunset of her life, she faced a new and devastating malady called dementia. A new kind of life was beginning.

It all began with her diagnosis of mild cognitive impairment (MCI). That came about when she began asking the same questions and doing the same things over and over. Or when she became disoriented about time and place (getting lost in the house, not finding the washroom, or roaming endlessly around the house like a caged squirrel looking for a way out). But a way out of which cage? She would get trapped in a corner of the bathroom and not be able to escape. Attempting to escape by turning around did not always succeed. She was now stuck on the floor inexorably facing a blank mirror.

"To what could be attributed this new malady afflicting Cosette?" I kept asking. Wasn't blindness bad enough? This was a new run of bad luck for us, and while we had chosen each other, now fate had chosen what was in store for us.

*   *   *

The first blow of what would become a series of sniping shots, came one day last summer when our daughter Charlene came visiting with her two girls, Bella and Stella, from Prince George, a town 800 kilometers north of Vancouver.

"Dad, there is something wrong with Mom. She keeps getting lost in the corridor; she can't find the washroom."

Soon after that we dined at Chez Michel one evening. During the day I had met with my friends. Anna, a journalist and writer and the wife of the Italian consul, and I discussed a proposal to write a book about the young Italo-Canadians of Vancouver: *The City of Future*. We discussed at length the subject of belonging, of the present and future generations' contacts with the existing Italian community. Both the consul and his wife were very keen on the undertaking of such a book, one that would reflect the realities of the times, vis-a-vis the much older and established generation of Italians in Vancouver.

Sitting on the sun-drenched balcony facing the beautiful Vancouver skyline on a Sunday afternoon, we discussed the initial plans for the project. The same day, after that most delightful dinner, Cosette and I returned home early, having left behind our friends, who were still enjoying a chat. On leaving the restaurant, Cosette unexpectedly said, "I don't know who some of these people are."

Incredulous, I thought that my wife was joking. Despite what my daughter had said earlier, I blamed her lack of vision for her problems. The thought that she might have difficulty remembering things never entered my mind, let alone that a more invasive illness might have entered hers. Then I recalled her recent confusion at home when she could not find her way quickly to the bathroom

"Where is the bathroom? I need to pee right now!"

Also, not being able to walk around the house and not knowing where she was.

"Where is the kitchen? Where is the sofa that I like so much for my naps?"

Suddenly she had forgotten the floor plan of our home, where we have lived for nearly forty years. I began asking new questions. "How do I provide a secure home environment to prevent her from getting hurt? Should I rearrange the furniture to give her better mobility?"

She had questions of her own: "Why have you moved the sofa, the chairs, the coffee table? I don't know my house anymore!"

But everything is as it was before. No furniture has changed.

Cosette also started forgetting dates and the time of day, our children's birthdays. A bombshell hit me. This is for real, I thought; something is happening to Cosette.

Shortly after, Dr. W. Smith, our family doctor, referred my wife to Dr. Komo, the Medical Director of the Geriatric Outreach Program-Assessment and Treatment of Vancouver Coastal Heath. Our first visit a few days later was one of general inquiries.

However, later in the program I was introduced to Becky Brechin, a nurse at the West Vancouver Adult Day Centre. Becky was kind enough to provide me with a copy of her newsletter article, entitled "Our Amazing Brain: Ways to Enhance Learning & Memory." In part here is what she writes:

Doctors, nurses and social workers assess or screen an older adult's immediate, recent and remote memory to ascertain their memory capabilities and potential need for supports to help maintain their independence in their community. They do this by asking people to remember a certain number of objects (often 3 objects, reciting a group of numbers, or inquiring about events that occurred within the last 24 to 48 hours, etc. To elicit remote memory, they may ask about significant life events that occurred years ago, such as a wedding anniversary, where you vacationed, your kids and grandkids names, etc.

Memory is one of five main cognitive functions (mental processing). The others include attention (as to detail), language (as in writing sentences, verbally repeating a sentence, visual – spatial skills, like your mind's eye which sees images of where you are going, which is very necessary in getting from one place to another, and executive functioning. Working memory is the foundation of the brain's executive functioning.

As I sat beside a confused Cosette in a tiny room barely large enough to accommodate four people in the presence of a registered physiotherapist, my wife was tested for her physical health and mental abilities. Another visit followed with cognitive and memory tests, plus skill tests regarding her mobility. Most of these tests took place in our living room. The tests were fairly simple ones, like putting a square block in the proper space on a board. Others concerned memory, like remembering dates and names. Did she know the year, season, month, date, the day of the week?

"Where are we?" asked the nurse. "Which country, province, city, office, floor?

"Mrs. Rocca, I am going to name three objects. I want you memorize them. I will ask you later for these same words to see if you can remember them. The objects are: pencil, watch, paper.

"Mrs. Rocca, how old are you?"

"I am seventy or something. Seventy-one."

Cosette was seventy-four. I started to laugh. "Really?" But soon I kept silent. I must not interfere. My time to be helpful would come later.

"How old are your children?"

"I am not quite sure. Forty-two and Forty-three?"

"What are their birthdays?"

"The months and dates?"

"Yes, the months and dates," the physiotherapist replied softly.

"February and, I think, October."

"Good!" The physiotherapist continued. "And the dates?"

She shook her head.

"Mrs. Rocca, can you spell the word 'world'?"

"W-o-r-l-d."

"Good. Now spell it backwards."

"Backwards?" Cosette began to tighten up.

"D-o-l... I can't," she said.

"Can you draw a square on this piece of paper?" A black sheet of paper was put before her.

"Where? How? I can't see. You know I am blind!"

"Sorry. Just try... if you can remember."

"Why I am being asked all these questions?" Cosette finally burst out.

"It's OK, dear. It's just a game." I soon regretted the word "game."

"A game? You call this a game? You are asking me all these stupid questions and you call it a game? You, Marc, and... these people? Who are they?"

But soon an attempt was made to draw the shape. The square became a tangle of flying lines in V-formation, but inverted and going nowhere on the white paper.

"Now what about a circle? Can you draw a circle?"

Squiggles appeared on the paper.

"Mrs. Rocca, do you remember the three objects I read to you at the start of this meeting?"

"Pen, something... clock... I don't know."

"Repeat: no ifs, ands, or buts."

"What kind of a question is that?"

"OK for now. I am sorry that your vision impairment makes the tests more difficult, but I think I have enough to complete this test. End of session for now," announced the physiotherapist. She had done most of the testing to determine Cosette's cognitive level using a mini mental state examination.

In his report, Dr. Como stated, "She scored 14/21 on the first items, and then she got 1/3 on recall, got 1 with cueing and could not get the other one. She had a hard time describing where the numbers on a clock would be and could not describe where the hands would go to show 10 past 11. Neurologically, she is pretty intact besides she is blind."

"I will be sending you another lady; she is a pharmacist. She will review all the prescriptions you're taking."

From then on there would be a procession of specialists from the Vancouver Coastal Health Outreach Program streaming in and out of our home. Two days later Ms. Desjardins called. She reviewed the medication and recommended that a dosette be used for the dispensation.

Next on the list, on July 5, 2012, the dietician reviewed several products with us to purchase: Caltrate soft chew candies, 650 mg/calcium/ tablets/ one a day. High calorie yogurt 6 % MF. Tylenol extra strength 500 mg for neck pain. Vitamin D 1000 units, one tablet daily.

The procession continued with another therapist to complete the assessment. Our bathroom needed upgrading for Cosette's bathing needs: install 12``X

24`` knurled stainless steel grab bars. Buy bath stool with back.

The final report by Dr. Komo was waiting for us a few days later when I arrived, this time in the company of our two daughters, Charlene and Martha. I wanted them to be there to hear directly from the doctor the verdict about their mother. This time I left Cosette home in the care of our granddaughters, Bella and Stella, to look after their nonna. Bella is fifteen, with dark gold hair, and Stella is eleven, vivacious and with light blond hair. Both girls are adorable. Although happy to be with them, my wife earlier became visibly upset when she found out she would be excluded from the meeting regarding the decision-making that would affect her life. These decisions were being made without her, and she wasn't happy about it.

"If it's about me, I should be there," she insisted. "What is there that I should not know?"

For me it was important that our daughters be there because we would be sparing my wife the ugly diagnosis of dementia, and especially the planning about what to do in front of her.

As we sat listening to the doctor, the report was first handed to me to read. Not having enough time, I passed it to my daughter Charlene, who glanced over it then passed it to Martha. Martha is the health worker in the family.

The key points of the report were not encouraging and left no doubt about the diagnosis. All the enervating medical issues affecting Cosette emerged as a new fact of life: a diagnosis of mild cognitive impairment. When we got back home, Cosette drilled our daughters about her not being with them at the doctor. Charlene tried to reassure her mother that things would work out well. Dad would take care of her mother as he always did. However, she tried to explain that she should not be counted on for being of any use as she lived far away north, a good eight-hour drive from Vancouver. It would be highly unlikely that she would be capable of providing her mother any support.

On the other hand, Martha cried her heart out with promises to do anything and everything for her mother. Embroiled as she was with a custody battle for her children, with endless court appearances, I discounted her ability to provide any support for her mother.

"Let's face it, Martha. As things now stand, your mom and I have had a hard time tracking down what you do. Despite the large pool of tears you have shed so far, I don't think for a moment that you would be able to offer any help. Besides, when was the last time you invited us to your home? If I remember correctly, it's been six years since you bought the townhouse, and we haven't been in it."

As if that wasn't enough, Charlene, excusing herself from filial piety, said, "Dad? Please, Dad, I don't intend to be disrespectful, but Mom has been under your care since she became blind. You have done a super job caring for Mom, but now you must continue to care for her the best you can. I know it is a stressful situation for you, but please continue to do your best."

It seemed that our offspring did not want to have anything to do with their mother's dementia. This solemn proclamation spoke complimentary words that inflicted invisible wounds nevertheless. Without any reservations, their mother was my responsibility and my preoccupation, as it always was. That I know. I also know that I married their mother for better or for worse. But I knew all too well the difficulty the girls faced. One was the distance: our daughters both lived far away. Also, they had their own problems—one more than the other. The health worker had a job with an impossible work schedule, and the visits with her girls were made difficult by her estranged husband. The other, a mother of two schoolchildren, only had occasional part-time employment, which required travelling in the region. Also, her husband had found a new job a two-hour drive from home. It was impractical for them to have to deal with their mother.

"It's your problem, Dad." I repeated the words to myself in mocking self-pity.

In the end, it all came crashing down on my shoulders. I built up my shoulders going to work for my dad carrying mortar at the age of ten. When I finished school, I married and still shouldered many of the family's problems. My big shoulders, if they didn't fail me, should be strong enough to carry the load for the present and into the future. A new life of challenges and readjustments needed to be addressed. Our lives would never again be the same. Surrounded by fog, my plane vanished in the air.

"Will it land safely or explode in midair?" I kept asking myself as days became frightful and nights full of nightmares.

*　　*　　*

A few days after Cosette fainted, I visited Arlene at her apartment. Arlene had provided assistance to us on the Seawalk when my wife fainted. She gave me a booklet to read. The title was: *Just for YOU, for people diagnosed with Alzheimer Disease*, issued by the Alzheimer Society of Canada. Having dealt with her husband, who had the disease for a number of years, Arlene had some experience in dealing with dementia. In reality, the *YOU* in the title was really me, as I read to my blind wife. Dementia was described in the different stages of development.

From the report, I understood that Cosette was suffering from stage 5: early dementia. This revelation contradicted the information I had been given by our family doctor, who suggested she only had "Mild Cognitive Impairment" (MCI). But from stage 5, two more stages separated her from total incapacity and eventual placement in an extended care facility.

CHAPTER 2

The impact of dementia in Canada shows a sharp rise in the number of people affected with cognitive impairment. Almost 15% of people 65 and older are affected by it. It is estimated that this figure will double by the year 2030. The cost associated with the disease is presently estimated at $33 billion per year.

The statistics for the United States show relatively larger estimates of numbers and costs. On the site *alz.org*, we learn the quick facts, which show that 5.4 million Americans are living with Alzheimer's disease, and the cost to the nation is a staggering $200 billion: "The global impact of dementia is estimated at more that 35 million affected people. And the disease represents the most significant social and health crisis of this century." (5)

In a letter to a local newspaper, I read this comment: "Why is it then, that when a person loses cognitive abilities, they are no longer treated with dignity that should be offered to all persons?"

The list of the symptoms was long. If what I read from the published reports was right, Cosette suffered from far more than mild cognitive impairment, but was in the middle stage. The booklet further stated: "While the causes of Alzheimer disease are still unknown, the progression of the disease is well understood, it can be followed through a series of stages…" Dementia is a loss of brain function that occurs with certain diseases. Memory loss, confusion, suspicion, agitation, faulty thinking and judgement, and behavior are all signs of onset dementia.

For the moment, Cosette was coping with her double impairments of blindness and dementia. How long my caregiving would continue at home was guesswork. Most types of dementia are nonreversible. By now, the world knew that dealing with dementia was a heartbreaking task, and I had to deal with my wife all by myself. There were no shortcuts.

The note from the doctor, scribbled on a white pad, was:

Your husband will supervise your pill-taking. Use a dosette.

Start again on the 81mg ASA/Baby aspirin. Take in the morning.

Show your pharmacist all of the pills at your house.

Start taking the new medication each night.

For neck soreness, take 1000mg Tylenol (2 Ex. m4 illegible pills) and lie down.

Keep an event journal.

After two weeks, Dr. Komo prescribed a new medication: *Exelon Patch 5* with instructions to increase to *Exelon Patch 10,* double the power, after one month.

This medication is used for the treatment of the symptoms of patients with mild to moderate Alzheimer's diseases. The symptoms include progressive memory loss, increasing confusion and behavioral changes, as a result of which it becomes more and more difficult to carry out activities of daily living. An overdose with serious and life threatening side effects can happen if more than one patch at a time is applied. An overdose can cause severe nausea, diarrhea, high blood pressure, trouble breathing, slow heartbeat and fainting, seizure, increasing muscle weakness, and hallucinations. Most of these negative symptoms have occurred and keep reoccurring even when only one patch is used daily.

I began keeping notes of the daily difficulty Cosette faced with tasks that required abstract thinking, recording the things she said, her sudden outbursts and reactions concerning her life. The whole thing was unsettling, and by degrees the range of fear increased.

I started with item #6, jotting down a few observations regarding her behavior and her reaction to my concerns:

I tried to steer her away from another corner. "Watch out!" I cried, grabbing her by the arm. "You're going to fall down the stairs if you're not careful." My words fell on deaf ears. Pleading, I continued. "Turn to your right," I admonished her.

"This is my right," she snapped, waving her right hand and pointing it in front of her.

"I know, dear—that is your right hand, but you must turn ninety degrees to go right or you will fall."

She kept muttering something else while moving along and running her hand on the hallway wall to find the bathroom. "I know what I am doing. I wasn't born yesterday!" She lurched ahead.

I called her back, but thinking the better of it, I rushed to help her avoid the stairs and lead her to the bathroom. I managed to get hold of her just before she stepped off the top of the staircase.

"Let me out of here! You are not nice to me. This door was not here. You are changing all the doors in this house to imprison me." She repeats herself time and time again. "What time is it?"

"9:00 a.m. Your talking watch just told you. I did, too."

"What time do we go to the lawyer to sign the papers?"

At 3:00 p.m. I remind her.

"What time is it now?"

"9:02 a.m."

"I have to take a shower."

"I helped you shower earlier this morning."

"When is the care woman coming? She is late."

"She will be here tomorrow."

"What day is tomorrow?"

"Tuesday, Cosette. I've told you, Tuesday. Okay, sorry, but my patience is running thin."

"Tuesday. Okay, okay. Please don't shout. You never have enough patience with me."

"I am not shouting. I am just repeating the answers I gave to the questions you keep asking!"

"What day is today?"

"Today is Monday."

"And what day is tomorrow?"

"The woman comes on Tuesday at 12:30 p.m."

"She's supposed to come every day."

"Not every day. Only on Tuesday and Thursday."

She switched to something else kept at the back of her mind: our appointment with our lawyer later in the afternoon.

"Do I need photo IDs for the lawyer? You told me I need pictures."

"Your CNIB card and your Care Card have your picture on them."

"Ah! Where are they?"

"You carry them in your wallet with the other cards. The one you don't want me to touch. You tell me not to go though your 'things'."

"Where is my wallet?"

"It's in your purse."

"My purse? What purse?"

"The one in your closet. Where you keep all your personal cards."

"In the closet? Which closet?"

"The one in our bedroom."

She lived in another space and another dimension, both of which transported her back and forth in time. This house, where we have been living for nearly forty years, becomes that house, the one where we lived prior to moving here. She sees present happenings in terms of the past, so the present confuses her. To try to understand her world, I willingly join her in this cockeyed journey, where I become unreal myself by denying the obvious and going along with her. But entering her world that is mired in deception and strange wonderment does surely test me.

This is the reason she hides things in the most unlikely places. Or because… "Because I don't want you to find them," Cosette asserts. "This is my world. These are my closets and my drawers. You stay out."

Her closet—where she keeps, scores of dresses, suits, shoes, and purses, with many past purchases (some still in the original wrappings)—had always been her private domain that I was forbidden to enter. Her personal items in the drawers in our bedroom dresser took up most of the space. In her dresser, I only retained one drawer for myself. Most of my things were kept in a separate chest, and she kept those in order for me. Unfortunately, as she could not tend to herself anymore, I had to look for things that she needed. Circumstances dictated that I must assume the duty of purveyor of all things she owned, personal or not. But the jungle that I had to go through to find items for her was challenging, to say the least.

However, I must admit that, although visually impaired, during the last twenty-five years of her life, she managed to keep a system that helped her find her personal clothing with little effort. She knew which drawer in the dresser contained what: her bras, her stockings, and her underwear in one. Her socks, pajamas, sweaters, and slips in another. She placed these items neatly folded, so when required, she had no difficulty finding them. However, with the onset of her dementia, a new order was in place. The order became a disorder, thus finding things was guesswork.

She opened a drawer; she pulled out some garments and dropped them on the floor. She pulled out another drawer containing socks and stockings, some still in their plastic packages, and threw them on the bed. She was looking for something. "I can't find it," she said in anguish. "It must be here somewhere. Everything has been moved. This is not my home."

"Honey, what are you looking for?"

"I am looking for my girls' pictures, the ones you took yesterday."

"Firstly, I have not taken any pictures lately. Second, all the pictures are kept downstairs in the family room, not in your drawers. Third, they are of little use to you, so what's the point?" I tried to reason with her.

"Then take me there—I want to feel them in my hands, that's what I want to do. Darn it, Marc!"

She lost her temper again. I left the room to allow her to settle down, but what I saw when I came back to the bedroom was not an expectant hush, but a shamble I cannot describe. The carnage had continued in my absence: clothes off their hangers, shoeboxes opened and thrown off the shelves, expensive sweaters and cardigans dumped on the floor and looking like discarded pieces of clothing ready for the dumpsite. I feared having to face what might come next. Cosette had been a model wife and wonderful mother. Since I met her, she had been a class of her own for the family. She was truly remarkable. That perfection, however, was now lost.

The all-new Cosette was a person whose brain might be shriveling, and neurons disappearing. Were these new characteristics of "tangles and plaques," which researchers say are the hallmarks of Alzheimer's Disease?

"I am always in the dark. I don't know what's going on with me!" Her cry was heart-wrenching.

Even a mild contradiction would shatter the peace. So far, I had only told my closest friends and family about the rages, the altercations. I could not keep everything to myself. My foreboding intensified. My silence simply suffocated me. I had to tell my children and my close friends about this precipice that surely would swallow me.

*   *   *

Although Dr. Komo's staff instructed me to use a dosette to dispense the prescription pills and tablets, I found this too cumbersome. Too many small plastic containers were involved to deal with.

This plan at times created confusion and sometimes resulted in me administering the wrong medication. To improve on this, the doctor decided to adopt compliance packaging, a practice in place in long-care pharmacies for years. This method was also becoming more common in community practice, as it offered efficiency and convenience. It also eliminated any possibility of errors, because the pharmacist assumed the responsibility and accountability for organizing the patient's medication. To address Cosette's cognitive impairment and to manage the large number of medications she was required to take, the pharmacist issued multi-medication blister cards with compartments representing the day of week and time, typically morning, noon, dinner, and evening. This arrangement would make things easier for me to administer the pills to my wife.

The idea to keep a journal would help me to record what was happening to Cosette. On the other hand, I was dealing with her illness all alone, and I was not too keen on recording anything yet. It pained me to think about it. My mind was already strained to see the car running out of control and going down the wrong way. But I was powerless to stop it; I was not at the wheel myself and, figuratively speaking, suddenly applying the brake would complicate matters. I could just read the headlines in the paper "Husband tries to stop the car at whose wheel is this thing called 'dementia'."

*   *   *

It was a balmy October afternoon in 2012 when I took Cosette for a walk along West Vancouver's waterfront. My wife was in remarkably and unusually good spirits when we entered the park. She wore her favorite fish-scale turtleneck sweater and light three-quarter-length navy-blue coat. Walking under the tall cottonwood trees already in autumnal colors, I looked upward to the herons' nests in the treetops. The migratory wading birds have long slender legs, long necks, and tapering pointed bills.

"They are funny looking things these birds, don't you think?" I remarked casually. My comment was answered with laughter.

"Why don't you put makeup on them so they can look prettier—like flamingos?"

Amazed at the remark, I burst into hilarious laughter that resonated around us on the trail. I hugged my wife close and continued to walk westerly along the waterfront to the pier. Enjoying the last of the October sun, pedestrian crowds were on the Seawalk, some clustering here and there chatting. Mothers and nannies were pushing babies in strollers. People held leashes while their dogs ran along the other side of the fence. The ocean waves gently lapped the breakwater along the water's edge. A couple of kayaks slid by silently into the late afternoon, and a shiny seal with inquiring eyes popped up from the mirror of the bay. In the distance, a number of cargo ships lay at anchor in the harbor. From where I had parked the car to the Dundarave pier is a distance of about two kilometers. On the way back from our stroll, Cosette began to slow down, breathing hard and perspiring. Her heart was racing. Turning close to me, she whispered.

"I'm dizzy, I need to rest."

We stopped and sat on a bench nearby. I felt her forehead: she was on fire. To let her cool down, we stopped briefly, then soon after we resumed our walk, with Cosette going at a leaden pace. Only a few yards away, she began trembling again.

"Marc, let's stop," she said, this time barely audible.

She nearly passed out on the way to the next bench. I supported her limp body. A woman strolling by approached and took Cosette's pulse. My wife's heart was racing, so the woman asked passersby for water. Two people offered their water bottles. After a short rest, Cosette seemed to recover and once again we resumed our walk. I held her tight to my side, praying that we would soon reach the parking lot and get to our car, but that was still some distance away.

The third time Cosette faltered, she reclined her head on my shoulder. Her legs felt rubbery against mine. This time I could not hold her up, but help came when someone rushed over to us. Soon a crowd of onlookers gathered. Someone was calling 911 for an ambulance. While we waited a wonderful Samaritan, Arlene, the first volunteer, introduced herself and offered to help. She rubbed Cosette's hands, sprinkled water on her forehead, and kept her from passing out until the ambulance arrived. Arlene instructed the ambulance driver by telephone to wait at the bottom of 24th Street and send a stretcher to pick up my wife, who was lying on a bench about a block away.

The ordeal had worried me. Afterwards, while still trying to reassure me, Arlene drove me to my car parked at the bottom of the 17th Street parking lot by John Lawson Park.

At the hospital, I found my wife on a stretcher in one of the corridors in the triage area, waiting to be transferred to an observation room. We waited there for over two hours before Cosette was wired up to an intravenous machine. Later, another nurse took blood from her. She was kept under surveillance for an unsettlingly long time.

After the results of the blood tests were known, the attending physician, Dr. O'Neal, gave me the shocking news that my wife had suffered a heart attack. He soon followed with the words, "She's being transferred to the Cardiology Department for more tests to be sure."

A nurse removed the needle from Cosette's arm, which had turned black and blue (the previous nurse had botched inserting the needle the first time), and then wheeled Cosette away on a stretcher for an electrocardiograph. Much later, gleaning bits of information and support online, I learned that the test he was referring to was a myocardial perfusion scan. (4)

A myocardial perfusion scan uses a special chemical called radionuclide. A radionuclide or isotope is a chemical that emits a type of radioactivity called gamma rays. In a myocardial perfusion scan, a tiny amount of radionuclide is put into the body, usually by injecting it into a vein.

For a moment I stared blankly at the doctor, who quickly left. I felt weak and thought I was going to pass out. Speechless, I returned to Cosette's bedside. Bending down, I kissed her forehead tenderly. Not wishing to worry her unnecessarily, I refrained from saying too much else, knowing full well that the hospital staff needed to take more tests, scheduled for 7 a.m. the following morning.

When I saw my wife again the next morning, I felt a strong need to cry. She was plastered with electrodes on her chest. The electrodes were connected to a machine that would show how the heart was responding. Seemingly quite alert, when Cosette saw me, she quipped, "Welcome to the 'bionic woman.'"

My wife appeared to be in unusually good spirits, and I thought, "Gee, thank God. Despite all, my wife still has a sense of humor," and I breathed a sigh of relief.

The day after the scan, the cardiologist, Dr. John R. Imrie, informed me by telephone. "The results of your wife's tests show no signs of a hardening of the arteries and no evidence of any strokes. So no poor blood supply exists due to narrowed coronary arteries that may have been damaged by a heart attack. For the moment, your wife is out of danger. A full report will be sent to your family doctor."

Later it was suggested that she might have had CHF (congestive heart failure), a condition in which the heart cannot pump enough blood to meet the needs of the body.

"Heart failure occurs after the heart muscle has been damaged or weakened by another primary cause, such as high blood pressure, coronary artery disease, or certain kinds of infections." (13)

In the next couple of days, a visit to our family doctor would prove that everything looked fine. However, when I asked him what was causing the frequent fainting spells, I also asked, "What else was wrong with Cosette?"

But there was nothing new he could tell us. We were still in limbo, and we wondered if the doctor was telling us the truth about my wife. Was the unexplained chest pain a result of too much exercise? Cosette had been instructed to exercise every day for one hour. Was the walk that day too stressful for her, causing her to pass out? Or was it the result of too much of the medication she was taking? Or were the side effects from the Exelon* Patch 10 (Rivastigmine Transdermal Patch)?

The news on her dementia was not encouraging either. "Did my wife suffer a heart attack, or did she have a cardiac arrest?"

The cardiologist said no.

Was my wife at level 5 on the dementia scale, as suggested Dr. Komo, or another level (cognitive impairment)? I did some research of my own. In one report I read this line: "Dementia also can be due to many strokes, This is called vascular dementia."

I needed answers to these questions. On the morning of November 23, I telephoned the family doctor's office, requesting copies of the reports in question. I did not know that I was asking for something impossible. Much later the same day, while Cosette and I were having dinner, the telephone rang. It was the family doctor W. Smith calling. I was quite taken aback by the doctor's message and the tone of his voice. What the doctor said was, more or less, "No. You cannot have copies of the reports. These are addressed to me, and they are for my sole discretion and you are not entitled to them. If you have power of attorney over your wife, you can request the reports directly from the specialists involved." End of conversation.

I was left holding the silent phone in my hand, dismissed and feeling foolish. However, I knew very well that the doctor was referring to the wrong document. What I required was the power given to me by Cosette in the nomination of committee, which states in part "… I nominate my husband … if I become incapable of managing my affairs, incapable of managing myself, or incapable of managing myself and my affairs." I was in fact the nominee in her testament, so I had every right to ask questions on her behalf.

Nevertheless, after the cardiologist's telephone call, I was reassured that at last we could sail away on the Zaandam of the Holland America Line for Hawaii. I had booked a cruise to the islands to celebrate Cosette's birthday. We were scheduled to board the ship on the 23rd of October, the day when the swallows leave San Juan Capistrano to return each spring, amid church bells ringing, to the old ruins of the mission.

Reassured that we would not require more medical insurance than we already had, we sailed for

San Diego, California. Sadly, our return proved to be an event not so glorious, as the only bells ringing in my ears were the words that the doctor had pronounced after Cosette had become incoherent again: dementia, dementia, dementia. Soon after the visit to our doctor, my wife began to act strangely daily, and I was once again shaken.

For example, Cosette would not leave the house to go to church one Sunday morning because of an odd demand. "I need my wig," she kept telling me. "I will not go unless you find it." And then turning to me, distressed, she demanded, "Find my wig, or I will not go. You always lose my things. Don't you see? I am losing all my hair!" she shouted accusingly.

"Do not worry," I replied, "I will buy you a new one. How about that?"

Cosette did not own a wig, but in her strange state of mind she was convinced she did. These flare-ups occurred quite frequently and unexpectedly. Her life had changed from one of total blindness to a topsy-turvy black world of disorientation. She had adjusted to the shapes of the physical world around herself to have a modicum of self assurance, but now she had lost that also, and there was no way of going back. Since the onset of her total blindness, things around her were recognizable by touch. Her movements had directions, but now she was lost in the fog of her new self. Her brain functioned like an electric bulb switching on and off. Space no longer existed, and clouds swirled around her as she attempted to touch them and hold on to them. Her world had dissipated in a vacuum. Now she stared blankly at the double darkness of her life: the intangible fears and confusion.

I pondered the problem I was facing. I could not reverse her problems, just like rivers can't go back to their sources and volcanoes can't recede into their mountains. The die was cast, the mold was shattered, and my life was now topsy-turvy. What had happened to my gentle wife?

CHAPTER 3

That late October day, Cosette and I were to board the cruise ship Zandaam for Hawaii, I picked up my car at the Honda garage. The day before, my new Honda Accord had developed some unexpected problems with an electronic switch and needed servicing. The required part had been ordered from the Calgary Honda service department and had been sent overnight to the shop. The car was ready only a few hours prior to our departure for the cruise terminal. My friend John C. drove us to the cruise ship terminal in downtown Vancouver. Considering that it was rush hour, we encountered few problems. As I guided my friend through the underground parking area of the building, John wondered, "This area has been redeveloped so much I can hardly recognize it. Where do I go from here?"

John had never driven to the new cavernous belly of Canada Place before. As Cosette required wheelchair assistance, she was quickly expedited on board, while I scurried behind carrying the hand luggage. Once aboard, we settled comfortably in our cabin.

After four days at sea we docked in San Diego, California. While the ship was in port for a scheduled few-hours stop, Cosette and I went shopping. We had planned on buying some extra clothing that I had forgotten to pack. We exited the ship and proceeded to US Customs with our passports in hand. Once outside the terminal I intended to hire a taxi, but an attendant suggested that we hop on a rickshaw (a pedicab) manned by a young Puerto Rican man. The chap was talkative and informative, acting as a sort of guide along the way. However, it seemed that he was heading the wrong way. Not that his travelers knew exactly where to go in San Diego to buy the undergarments I had forgotten to pack, but the guide was heading to the souvenir shop by the Seaport Village located a short distance from the Midway Museum, an area along the Embarcadero.

"Stop!" I spoke out, "It's not souvenirs we need but to visit a shopping mall. Please take us where there is a Macy's store."

The driver stopped, turned around, and, dodging the traffic along Harbor Drive and then along Market Street, delivered us in front of the Horton Plaza.

"How much?" I asked the Puerto Rican.

"Forty bucks. It's a long way from the cruise ship terminal."

Visibly upset about the amount demanded, I blurted out, "Are you kidding me?" Blaming myself for not negotiating the fare beforehand, I said, "Here is thirty. Count yourself lucky," and handed him the twenty-dollar bill I had planned to give him plus a ten-dollar tip. We jumped off and left to do our shopping. After visiting the mall, I flagged a taxi to take us back to the ship. The taxi fare for the return trip to the ship came to only seven dollars. Now I knew that the Puerto Rican had taken us on an expensive ride.

October 29, 2012, it seemed that we leapt out of San Diego for the open Pacific Ocean on the wings of an albatross. We enjoyed the first warm weather as the ship crossed the 120 meridian on our way to Hawaii. But hardly had the blanket of blue sky lifted when a cold dark cloud set in.

The next day, while sunbathing on the pool deck, I was notified by the ship's captain's office that I was to receive an urgent telephone call from home. The call would come to our cabin, the stateroom. This message cast dread in my heart. What could be so urgent to require contacting me in the middle of the Pacific Ocean? Did something sinister happen to one of our daughters or our grandchildren? Was someone hurt so badly that we needed to return home? Needless to say, waiting for the next call was worrying, and Cosette began showing signs of extreme discomfort. When the call was finally put through, it was our daughter Charlene informing me that my car had been stolen from our carport as soon as we left for the cruise terminal. Although at the time the news sounded dire, I dismissed the need for urgency. However, that call threw Cosette into despair. I asked for details of what had happened. I was told that the police were called and a report about the incident was made for future reference. In the end, I told my daughter that I would deal with matter upon our return home and not to worry so much as the car was insured. The next night Cosette became concerned at the thought that the thief might have entered the house when our car was stolen.

Ever since we were the victims of a break-in many years ago in our first house in East Vancouver, and a year ago when there was a break-in in our house in France, Cosette had always felt unsafe. She became obsessed, and since then she has kept every exterior door locked at all times.

One night she hallucinated that the bus on which we were riding was about to crash. She rose abruptly and braced for it in the darkness, then she screamed. I held her in my arms and tried to calm her down. She resisted me at first—I was the intruder—then slowly she regained her composure and resumed her sleep. But later, she woke up whispering, "Where is Martha? I want to see my Martha. Why doesn't she come to see me?" She was agitated now. I tried to reassure her that our daughter had telephoned to say hi, but could not come. The next day she did not remember having dreamed at all.

When worries were too great for me to bear, I would find solace in the garden. There I always had things to do. With a large pool and terraced lawns, fruit trees, and shrubs, I could spend hours busying myself in the open air and was always within earshot if Cosette needed me. And during rainy days I would retire to the study to write, but I was on a cruise ship now. Where would I relax in the next two weeks? There was no escape, no jumping off the Zaandam to go home. My only resolve was to look at the problem squarely in the face and deal with it. To me the potential loss of the car was something that I could deal with on our return home. Discounting the urgency of the matter, I resolved to make the best of the time on the cruise and enjoy every minute of it. But at first I had to reassure my wife that nothing was so grave for us not to enjoy the planned visits to various Hawaiian Islands.

CHAPTER 4

After our return from our cruise, I had every reason to be under stress. Taking care of someone with dementia requires time and energy. It can be a demanding and stressful task. To add to that, only a short while had passed since I had attended my brother's funeral. Under heavy sedation, Nando's last days were spent in peace and with dignity, surrounded by his siblings. I felt a strong kinship with my mentally challenged brother. The family had entrusted my brother to me for many years, and when he finally departed this world, the loss was accepted with resignation. My brother's life had not been one of comfort and happiness. That chapter was now closed, but others would soon open and challenge my very fabric and enduring self-assurance.

Where at first I determinedly dealt with unforeseen problems, now everything loomed like mountains. The problems with Cosette's health, my dental surgery, and my worries about the prostate biopsy to check for evidence of cancer all conspired to add oil to the fire. My presence of mind began to falter. I recited to myself, "I cannot scale this mountain alone and must, at all costs, at least find a path through the forest that leads to it."

In the last few years, I had a foreboding that something sinister would happen to me, something intangible and difficult to describe. It is a sensation that invades one's body and pervades it like a rash or shingles, leaving the body like gooseflesh. All of that leaves one with a sense of incapacity that one cannot dust away. My fears had magnified in the last few months.

Dreams. I dreamed strange dreams filled with dread and foreboding. One night I dreamt that my wife was walking by a fast-flowing canal and dragging our youngest daughter Martha along. The child was screaming and resisting by pulling to and fro. Unexpectedly a car drove by at full speed, striking our child and hurling her into the canal. The dream had a chilling effect on me. I jumped up with tears in my eyes. Afterwards I could not make sense of that horrible nightmare. However, I had another more sinister dream, one where I was about to drown myself in the pool. But before I could do so, my wife approached from behind, calling me all sorts of names—weak and selfish.

Enraged, I grabbed my wife and pushed her into the pool. My wife could not swim. Surely she would drown. Remorseful about what I have just done, I flung myself into the water to save her from drowning. All these strange dreams were a blend of the surreal, at odds with the real world around me. The stress going on in my mind was playing tricks. All was topsy-turvy in my life. I loved my wife immensely, so why such horrible dreams?

In her unstable state, she repeatedly called me nasty names, but she could not distinguish good from bad or real from imagined. I have read that attacks like these are common for dementia patients, so I accepted what came to me.

One day, remarking on the barbs that were thrown at me by Cosette from time to time, I said to myself, "I get stoned every day—not the kind that comes out of a good bottle, but the kind that comes out of a sick mouth." No sooner had the thought crossed my mind than I regretted it.

Truly, Cosette's health problems started to take a turn for the worse at the time of Martha's divorce seven years ago. In an affidavit by the defendant to the court, our daughter's husband made the vilest insinuation against us, accusing us of having been "… physically abusive to her as a child, and the abuse continued until she was a teenager." What brought about that flaming lie on the part of her estranged husband? And worse still, unspeakable and serious accusations were written against me. Our ex-son-in-law would use all malicious ways to win in court. Both accusations were false and devastating to bear, especially for Cosette. There are sick people on this earth whose sole purpose in life is to destroy other people's lives. He treated his wife—and continued to do so in court and elsewhere—like an object that needed to be totally crushed.

Needless to say, our daughter's separation had been a bitter contest that involved the courts and the church as well. At the end, on religious grounds the church did not recognize the annulment, a fact disputed vigorously by her husband. However, our daughter's marriage stood in the eyes of the church as advised in a letter from the Vancouver Regional Tribunal. Their decision as reported was, "This is to advise you that the Judges in session … rendered a *Negative* decision; that is, they have not found your marriage to be proven to be invalid according to the grounds alleged. Thus, the presumption of law that your marriage is valid, remains."

The decision suited our daughter, but things got much worse for her, as her ex-husband had sought the annulment to remarry a third time to no avail. Their marriage proved to be a bitter union of two Catholic people at the opposite sides of the scale of human tragedy: one, a born Catholic; the other, a born-again Christian, ill-bent on adding to human suffering. Every time our daughter was dragged back to court, it became a never-ending soccer game, the ball kicked back and forth. When the ball ended in the net the glory went to scorer, the kicker, and the ball ultimately was placed again in center field to be kicked all over again. Unfortunately, the judicial system allows such futile and vicious hassles—really harassment—to be played in court. These games are expensive and take a heavy toll on the spouses, the children, and grandparents as well. Tragically, the separation has taken a heavy toll, especially on poor Cosette. The wound was still open, not quite healed. It still bled, and we were powerless to do anything about the sad situation.

For us, gone were the sweet dreams of youth when all was green and pastoral, and where rivers flew silent, and the blue sky dominated the roof of the world. As were later times when we married and were happy as newlyweds. The world had danced around us, and we had rejoiced in it. We were happy then. Surrounded by each other and our two daughters, we worked hard, made sacrifices, and at times we worried when things did not go our way. And yes, like other people coming to a new country, we did have a care in the world. Now the lark's song was silent, and my face and eyes had lost their sheen. The whiskers on my face were a stubble of white. The texture of my skin, especially my hands, started to look like parchment paper. I did not ask for pleasant dreams anymore, only to be left alone with my solitude. The life of darkness and dementia of my wife kept me company both day and night.

PART TWO

CHAPTER 5

I had just turned twenty when I met Cosette on
the pebble beach of Villefranche Sur Mer on the
splendid Cote D'Azure, France. I was a student
from Italy taking courses at the Université Sophia
Antipolis. I had enrolled in engineering classes. On
the beach one day, looking out at the sailboats in the
bay, I craned my head to look at a girl wearing a red-
and-white-striped bathing suit and sporting dark
sunglasses. She was sitting on a straw mat with an
open book in her hands. I instantly took a fancy to
her, and I could not rid myself of the vision of her.
She told me later that she was on a break from her
studies to become a nurse. And there I was, not far
away, squatting down on the smooth, shiny pebbles

while puffing on a Gitane cigarette, which I held between the two forefingers of my left hand, my thumb resting on my shoulder. With my right hand I played ducks and drakes, trying to skim flat stones in the water. I had not changed into a bathing suit yet. I was mindful about my skinny body. I was timid to show my spindly legs, especially when pretty girls were around. Slowly and still in a squatted position, I moved closer to the girl.

Noticing the odd glances that l'etranger, cast in her direction from time to time, Cosette folded her book and peered over her sunglasses, following my unorthodox movements. I finally gained enough boldness to make a move. Gambling with my heart, I stood up, holding a small flat stone in my hand. I made a wish and threw the stone on the surface of the water. If the stone skipped over the water's surface, I would approach the girl. Luckily, the stone skipped twice. Seizing the moment, I made my move.

I walked towards the girl, the clatter of pebbles under my feet. I moved closer, addressing her in French. "*Toute seule?*"

She was by herself. Realizing I had said something rather silly, I corrected myself. "*Bonjour!*" I blurted out.

Surprised, she laughed at my first attempts to get her attention, but she soon responded with a kind smile and politely invited me to join her. Accepting, I timidly squatted beside her on the mat.

Her eyes under the tinted glasses appeared bright, but I could not read through them. Her hands were long and delicate. The colour of her skin was unusually fair, and I thought she might be Nordic. This observation was reinforced by her invitation to sit beside her. However, this observation would soon fade away.

Noting the book she was reading I asked her, "Do you like *L'Etranger?*"

She smiled. She removed her glasses, showing her dark shiny eyes. "You mean Camus?"

Next I asked her name.

"*Cosette. Je m'appelle Cosette.,*" she replied with a marked and sensuous Meridional French accent.

"Ah, the name of the girl in *Les Miserables.* I like the name. I read the book by Victor Hugo," I was quick to boast.

Pleased about the compliment, Cosette asked, "And you? What is your name?"

"My name is Marco."

"*Ah, Marc!*" She rolled the **"R"** in her throat.

"Do you come here often?" I asked.

"Sometimes, when I have a break from my studies," she replied.

Next I wanted to know if she liked what she was reading, and I boldly popped another question.

"Cosette, what do you think about Camus's writings? Myself, I have been reading J.P. Sartre lately. *The Age of Reason.*" (7)

Studying this Italian young man for a moment, Cosette finally offered her opinion on the two very popular writers of the time. "Camus embraced life, and friendship is what Albert Camus based his life on. J.P. Sartre, on the other hand, embraced Marxism and viewed life in a more existentialist way." In closing she added, "Camus had a falling out with Sartre over their different perspectives on life."

I wondered if she was talking about his lifelong relationship with Simone de Beauvoir, who was known as one of the forerunning feminists writing at the time, and she had other lovers, both male and female. Cosette, by contrast, only later felt the need to be feminist in her life. Oddly though, Cosette had read and liked the novel *Bonjour Tristesse* by Francoise Sagan, who was born in 1935, the same year as me.

I was impressed with her apparent knowledge of popular French writers of the times. I smiled with contentment and switched subjects to French movies and the popular actors of the day.

"Who is the French actor you like the most?" I asked.

"I adore Jean-Paul Belmondo! He is of Italian descent, you know?" She replied straightaway.

"His father was born in Algeria of Italian parents," I corrected her.

We had a minor disagreement when I revealed my preference. "Alain Delon is my idol. I compare him to the American actor James Dean. Delon is more handsome than Belmondo, and I like his voice better."

She responded by asking me about my favorite French actress.

"Catherine Deneuve," I replied without hesitation.

"I agree," she said. "I like her over Brigitte Bardot."

We connected right away. A pleasant demeanor pervaded her being. The conviction of her beliefs and her cultured manners, as revealed in further discussions, convinced me that I might have found a soulmate. I would always regard Cosette as a well-learned person. A person to be loved.

That day, after we met, she drove me back on her new 1955 Vespa scooter to my home-stay in the center of town. Was I happy sitting behind her and holding on to her! With the wind in our faces, we left the beach for the bustle of the district where my parents were paying room and board. I loved the sensation of riding through the narrow streets lined with small cafes with their yellow and white marquees. I was extremely happy to have met a smart, lovely girl with black hair and big brown eyes. After she let me off in front of my residence, she revved up her machine and sped off, saying with a promising and joyous smile, *"Au revoir. A la prochaine, Marc!"*

She loved her scooter. It was her only possession, bought with her earnings working in her spare time as a governess.

That was the beginning of an encounter that would last to this day. We kept seeing each other during the school year. At every opportunity we stole time to be together whenever possible. Riding her Vespa up and down the steep and narrow streets of Villefrance and beyond with me latched up behind her, she took me to visit many places that I had not been before. For me, it was an exhilarating experience. Cosette owned a Vespa! I had always dreamed to own one. But I was too poor. It was hard enough for my parents to send me to school in France and pay for room-and-board, let alone provide me with a scooter. I couldn't even afford a bike, let alone a Vespa. I felt on cloud 9.

Before meeting Cosette I had issues with negative views of life. She showed me the sights of the region, which was rich and beautiful with the history of the land and its people. The many jaunts to nearby Nice and Monaco, Monte Carlo, and many country roads and villages along the coast were a learning experience for me, and they planted deep seeds of affection for the girl I would soon fall in love with and marry. I took to Cosette like a duck takes to water. She was my real true love. I spent more time studying her than my assigned Engineering studies.

One weekend we traveled by scooter to Ventimiglia and San Remo in Italy. In a restaurant we ordered pasta with tomato sauce and meatballs. Cosette liked Italian food, and she kept asking for more bread so she could dip it in the meat sauce—a common practice in rural Italy, which would stay with her even after we married and when she was invited to dine at my mother's house. This prompted the waiter to call her a *mangia pane,* a bread-lover. Ah, so much Italian bread and great homemade tomato sauce! She would never forget that.

Another time we scooted all the way to St Raphael and Frejus, where we visited an old Roman aqueduct, most of it only an imposing ruin. Nothing to compare with the Pont du Gard near Nimes or with the Roman Bridge at Vaison-la Romaine, but interesting to me nevertheless. I thought that my studies *sur place* in the bridge and canal architecture would one day benefit from such trips.

Ah, and the visit to Nimes. That was like redis-covering Rome and the Coliseum all over again. I felt a sense of belonging. After all, I had Roman blood in my veins. In Menton, where Cosette's best friend Michelle lived, we were chased out of the casino for being under the legal age. Undaunted, we bribed our way into a nearby cabaret that Michelle and her friend had suggested as being quite *ose'*. I attempted to dance while glued to Cosette, but I was unstable on my feet. I had tipped my elbow a bit too high above the normal that night. Alas! The French cognac and the Rosé I kept drinking that night finally caught up with me, with unpleasant results. Inebriated, I had to be accompanied back to Michelle's place on wobbly legs and was only allowed to sleep on a mattress placed on the kitchen floor, while Cosette slept in the spare bedroom.

When we returned to Villefranche, her father was furious. He accused us of elopement and banned Cosette from seeing this disgraceful Italian young man again. Her father's intransigence was a bit far-fetched—he had a grudge against Italians for siding with Hitler during WWII. Nevertheless, the banishment stood. But that did not matter to Cosette, as she had grown very fond of me and would not let go of me despite her father's stance. She had made a choice. Knowing full well that her father would never allow her to date an Italian, let alone marry him, she chose to leave her parents rather than have dictated to her whom she would marry. Besides, she was well aware that there would be no dowry from her parents and no financial help from mine.

The decision to elope did not come easy to either of us. A traditional marriage was out of the question. My parents would not allow me to quit school to marry an unknown French girl. Also, they were powerless to help their son financially any further, as they were recent immigrants to Canada and they lacked the funds. However, soon after pledging our love, we married in front of a justice of the peace in a simple civil ceremony at the city hall—*La Mairie*—with Michelle, who had traveled from Nice, and a roommate of mine at the Italian home-stay appearing as witnesses. Holding a small bouquet of lily of the valley in her left hand, with her hair made up in a lovely chignon by Michelle, Cosette appeared radiant and elegant in her dress. It was white with yellow polka dots. Around her waist she wore a red belt with golden eyelets that she still keeps, after so many years, in a drawer in our bedroom dresser. She wore a pair of white stiletto shoes *pour etre a la mode*: to be in fashion.

The ceremony was brief and dignified. Our vows were solemn and lasting, with a resounding "*Oui!*" from both of us. Our friends embraced and kissed us. Michelle had tears in her eyes. Cosette opened her arms to receive her embrace.

After working at odd jobs requiring no specific training (as we had not completed our studies), we struggled to make ends meet. I worked in a restaurant washing dishes, while Cosette was engaged as a governess. Yet our love kept us optimistic, even bold to find our way. After all, we had our love to support us in times of adversity.

At the time, opportunities abounded for immigrating to Canada. The quota for French nationals was high in those days. We found our way into the Canadian Consulate one day and applied to immigrate to Canada. Cosette and I, now husband and wife, had our paperwork expedited with the help of a Canadian businessman who had contacts at the Canadian Consulate in Villefranche. We boarded a ship out of Monaco bound for Montreal. In the new country we found work—not exactly what we had hoped for, but it gave us a start in our young lives. In Montreal I found work as an *arpenteur (*land-surveyor) with an engineering firm doing road layout.

The first two winters in La Belle Province proved to be too harsh, especially for Cosette, who was used to the climate of southern France. We left Montreal for Vancouver, where my parents resided in a working class district in East Vancouver's Little Italy.

Before Cosette would give birth to our first child (a girl), her parents finally accepted our invitation to visit. When the day arrived, they found a bitter winter with snow and a cold that would bite your fingertips and cut your breath, hardly the sort of climate one finds in Southern France. By coming to visit us, her parents forgave Cosette and welcomed the newborn with glee, but the experience of a cold winter left a nasty taste in their mouths. It was a long-drawn visit, and eventually, before their return to France, the sun would emerge to shine in our household. Now they knew that Vancouver was where Cosette would spend the rest of her life.

We worked hard. We lived frugally. We saved money and invested wisely. Our earlier frugality and sacrifices would later allow us to live comfortably in an upscale district in West Vancouver, once a staunch bastion of British exclusiveness. Here our daughters attended school, married, and moved away. Here is where we have been living in relative happiness, despite Cosette's visual impairment. That is, until other problems emerged from the murky waters of fate.

·

CHAPTER 6

Here it is important that I tell about our past, and Cosette's in particular. It is important because she needs to be reminded of her roots. As well, it is important for our grandchildren to know where she came from, who we were, and who we are now. Ever since Cosette came to this country she has not been alone, but she felt alienated from her family in France. Aside from my family and our few friends, she had no other family here in Vancouver. She has always been proud of her French upbringing and still is. But I wanted to know more. For many years I asked about her grandparents. To reopen a chapter of her life, we undertook many trips to her native country and discovered her true ancestry in Spain.

Cosette was born French, but everything else about her personality has pointed to a different background—one from Catalunia in Spain. Her name, medium height and build, black hair, flashing brown eyes, and her fierce retention of her identity were of Catalan lineage. Later in her life, I likened her to a Native wanting to remain Native.

Her diminutive maternal grandparents had migrated to France during the early nineteen hundreds. They came from Villafames, a picturesque village set high on the hills of Montenegre in the Valencia region. The town still remains entrenched in art and folklore and maintains its festivals, which attract thousands every year from the Benicassim seaside resort town of Oropensa Del Mar. Moreover, the village is characterized by the red rock formations in the region. Here, on top of a rocky outcrop is the ancient fortress, still in good condition, and the churches of the Asuncion and San Miguel y San Ramon. Cosette's grandmother walked long distances on foot across stony fields, carrying a child of three in a pouch hewn from sheepskins. At times making her way on horse-drawn carts used by the local peasants, Mrs. Mirailles finally rejoined her farmer/shepherd husband in Villar-en-Val in the Corbieres region. The Mirailles were hard-working and family-oriented. They raised three boys and two girls while scratching a living from a harsh land that one day would become rich in grapes and wine. Although the political situation in France was precarious, it was an improvement over what they had left behind in a poor Spanish village.

Cosette was two years old when WWII broke out. Soon after, France was invaded and occupied by Nazi forces. The country was divided in two parts for the duration of the war: one where a government (Vichy) was installed in collaboration with the Axis powers, and the other a government in exile in Algeria headed by General DeGaulle. Cosette's father, who was fighting with the Free French Army, was caught by the Germans and sent to work on a farm in Germany. Here he befriended another French prisoner from the Toulouse region. With Emile Puges he would cement a friendship that lasted a lifetime. That friendship would eventually transfer to both their respective children, a fact that is still in evidence to this day.

Cosette's father was born in Merens-les-Vals in the Ariege-Midi Pyrennees. Her paternal grandfather had roots in Puigcerdà (1), Catalunia. It was said, often in hushed tones, that her grandfather was a scoundrel and a drunkard. He worked on rock walls and did repair work for a local municipal works gang, hiring poor Catalan-speaking folks who could not read or write. He seldom paid his workers, preferring instead to squander his earnings on liquor and women. Disgracefully, he paid his lowly helpers by pimping his wife to them—workers who were as bestial as he was. After giving birth to a boy and a girl, the poor woman died, abused and destitute, at the age of thirty-four. But that did not stop this vulgar man from continuing the abuses, next molesting his teenaged daughter. By necessity the girl and her brother Jaime were placed under the tutelage of an aunt who ran a small inn in Puigcerdà next to the old church in the center of the town. After being banned by the family, the scoundrel disappeared from the memory of the surviving clan. Not a word was spoken of him for a long time. But he left a black mark on Cosette's father and his sister, Tante Moe. Even mentioning the grandfather's name was hushed up. "*C'est mieux de ne rien savoir*," Cosette was told whenever she asked questions. But time holds no secrets for the wrongdoer, and people would tell one day of the wicked man's morality, and those dark secrets would explode out of his grave.

By coincidence, Cosette only found out about her grandfather in 1987 when we traveled to Puigcerdà, the capital of the Catalan Comarca (district) de Cerdanya in the province of Girona. The daughter of a friend of the family, Arlette had invited Cosette and me to spend a few days in her mountain chalet high in the Cerdania District. The village lies high on the western flank of the Pyrennees in the shadow of Andorra principality.

Taking the D118, we left early one morning from Carcassonne, where Cosette's parents were living at the time, driving south in a small Peugeot borrowed from Cosette's father. We crossed Limoux, Couiza, and then Quillan. Staying on the same road, I reached Axat, where the road became narrower and climbed to a high plateau at 1700 meters above sea level, where we reached Mont-Louis. I veered right on the D618, and when the Peugeot had reached the foothills of the great Col de Puymorens, which stood at 2500 metres above sea level, we were in awe of the majestic Pyrenees. Here we stopped in Font Romeu and took a break in an alpine chalet used by members of the French Alpine Olympic Team for training; they were coached by a Canadian from Quebec. From there, the road veered to a steeper grade leading up to our destination: the town of Hur, where Cosette's friend Arlette lived. The next day our host introduced us to the town of Bourg Madame, and we later stopped in Puigcerdà for lunch.

During an afternoon stroll along the artificial lake fronting the cemetery, we met Pascal, a distant relative of Cosette's father, who had worked as a grave-digger in his youth at the same cemetery. When he learned of Cosette's family name, he cried out,

"Ah, I knew your grandmother. She also wore dark glasses. Your father Jaime as a young lad was quite a rebel. He had a rough time with your grandfather, though. Yes, your grandfather, *el borracho abusador,* the drunkard and abuser, is buried here," he told her.

The revelation came as a total shock to Cosette. She had no clue whatsoever about her grandfather, nor about his burial place. Anger built up momentarily within her, but anger about what? Why was she never told anything about her *grandpere?* The sky suddenly shattered open, revealing the dark secrets of her grandfather's life. She leaned over to my shoulder and, sobbing, felt an urge to enter the cemetery. As we pushed our way through a heavy rusted gate, a sudden chill came over Cosette as though the devil himself had put a hand over her shoulder. She thought better of it and asked me to walk away.

After our return to her parents' home, she related her visit to the cemetery to her father. He admitted that her grandfather was indeed buried in Puigcerdà but did not wish to say more about it, preferring to leave the matter dead. Only after her father's passing did a maternal aunt tell Cosette the whole gory story. Her grandfather's past had been dark and sealed,, but now his sins lay before her, an open-wound, deep and troubling. Alas, she did not know how to react. The memory of those revelations still haunted her, and she tried to forget.

Nevertheless, on many journeys throughout southern France and in Catalunia, Spain, Cosette and I enjoyed rambling through the countryside, exploring ancient castles and sacred abbeys, with their splendid churches and cultivated gardens. In times past, the abbeys were a vibrant nucleus of faith and work. Fervor and zeal no longer ruled within their walls, as many had been converted into museums. Often these journeys required taking chances on steep and narrow roadways to reach far-flung landmarks. The roads had been cut from old trails. As the car lurched forward on steep inclines, Cosette, with coy delight would ask me, "Where are you taking us today?"

My reply was never a surprise to her, as she was used to my strange choices.. "Following the ancient paths the monks took to spread the 'good word.' I think I can hear their sacred chants up ahead. And where the armies marched to do battle, I hear swordsmen fighting," I would reply.

These remarks were said jokingly, but were not always received in good humor by Cosette. Being inquisitive, I must have felt the energy emanating from these places, and my curiosity was the spark. She was afraid of heights and would not look down a ravine while in the car. Crisscrossing the many roads and villages, we came upon cemeteries dating back centuries. We searched and found old family names on stone crypts: Albert, Brunet, Catala, Colomer, Navarro, Palau, Pujol. And Cosette, exuding joy, was happy and thankful to me for having undertaken such a tour of discovery and contentment. With my wife by my side, we drove over mountain villages and scaled old castles on foot until our feet grew sore, but we would not give up. Spurred on by my desire for knowledge about the history of the regions and their people, we carried on farther and farther inland to the foothills of l'Alt Maestrat and la Torre d'en Besora in Catalonia. Then there was Morella, a fortress perched high on a hill a thousand metres above sea-level that is thought to be one of the first settlements in Spain. First settled by the Beribraces tribe when the Celts arrived in the fifth century BC, it was mentioned by Avieno (2) (3) in his *Ora Maritima:*

> *Ahi los Beribraces, tribu agreste*
> *Y feroz, vagaban entre los rebanos*
> *De su numeroso ganado. Ellos,*
> *Alimentandose pauperrimamente*
> *Con leche y pingue queso,*
> *Revelaban una vida semeante*
> *A los piedras.*

(Rough translation)

There the Beribraces, / agrarian tribes and fierce /
wandered among their sheep / in great herds, but
poorly feeding
themselves / on milk and fatty cheese. / They
revealed a life
similar to the stone age.

Ah, and not to forget Sagunto, which we
found beyond our expectations for its long and
tragic history. Coveted by the Romans and the
Carthaginians, the castle was destroyed in the
battles of the Second Punic War. Later it was par-
tially rebuilt with the aid of the Romans. After that
visit I dreamed of the old ruins, and I imagined
old battles being fought again amidst the breached
walls, while the fierce Iberian wind blew through
the cracks of history. Now I use memories of our
fascinating excursions to these ancient ruins, so full
of history, to ease my mind during my shut-in days
as a caregiver.

I have immense love for my wife in ways both
sensual and moral. In our early lives we made love
tenderly at home and while on vacation. But Cosette
always felt more reassured about her sexuality when
away from home, as if when she was away no one,
not even the walls, would witness her act of lovemaking. She was reserved in all her actions, being
shy and unpretentious.

"Hold my hand," she would plead with me, as if to say, "Don't let me go, ever." Holding her hand was more important to her than a kiss, making her feel protected. This way she felt the energy she needed to be reassured about her partner. At first Cosette was more spiritual and not too keen in experimenting with ways of lovemaking. Her love for me was the kind you don't boast about, and only rarely would she show amorous affection in front of other people. By and large I, the more carnal and self-indulgent of the two of us, had to adjust to her ways and never press on. Only occasionally would she accept my daring ways. At times she would wrap around herself a cloak of modesty, which suited her well, but often to my mild protestations. Regardless, our life together had been full of contentment.

I still remember with nostalgia those days of travel and discovery. On past visits to Cosette's ancestral hometown, I always took the low road trough Berriol. But one day, wishing to explore an old Roman ruin on our way to Villafames, I veered off Autopista Freeway A-7 above Platja del Mallo and headed for Cabares instead in the Plana Alta region. On the way, the road, lined with low-labored rock walls, became steep and winding. The countryside, although semidry and scrubby at that altitude, was laid out in spotted mountain pastures and circled by scrubby pines. Thyme grew wild in the region, and the pungent aroma filled the nostrils of the traveler. We felt on top of the world, and I loved to have my young wife by my side. On the way, I gazed at fig trees lining the road. I stopped the car and picked a few ripe figs to give Cosette. She remarked about the sweetness and delicacy of the fruit.

"Let's stay here and rest for a while; our reservation at the hotel can wait."

I stopped the car. I opened the trunk and extracted bread and goat cheese, uncorked a bottle of Rioja wine, and sat on a dry grassy spot under a large fig tree. This was a moment that brought us closer together. The warmth of the sun hugged us as we lay on the leafy ground. It all made us feel welcome and at ease. The overpowering aromatic odor of the thyme and the taste of the savory figs combined with the wine to work wonders on us— especially on Cosette.

"Marc, you know I can see with only one eye. The specialist told me that because of my glaucoma, I may lose the other eye. I want to remember you as you are now. I want to sculpt your face in my mind and in my heart before I lose the other." She gazed deeply into my eyes as she spoke.

"My love, this is paradise—we should be blessed for it. Let's consecrate this moment in our lives."

Unexpectedly, it seemed that she had cast all modesty to the wind. There were no walls around us, only the benign sky above. We were free and alone on top of the world. This was our life under the fig tree, our naked truth. Floating in happiness, we embraced the universe, lying naked and side-by-side, holding hands on a bed of dried fig leaves. It was as if we were planting roots again, this time in the land of her ancestors, and I was very much a part of it. Once again we pledged never to break faith with one another.

In the distance, the shimmering Mediterranean danced in a silky veil of violet, still and majestic. The sky had coalesced in heavenly blue, with not a cloud in sight. It was a memorable moment in our lives. One that we would cherish forever.

*   *   *

After we returned to France from our travels through southern Spain, I spoke to my father-in-law. We wished to buy out their house. We needed to have a more permanent base in France in proximity to Spain and Catalunia, where we could travel unimpeded. At first Cosette's parents appeared to be in agreement with the idea, but when the four of us were to meet at a notary public to sign the deed, Cosette's father did not show up. He had changed his mind about the whole thing. For many years we shelved our plans until later, when Mr. Palau passed away. Only then did the door open for another try. This time the proposal was made to Cosette's mother. Finally, when Cosette's mother became too ill to live in the house, we placed her in a home for seniors in Narbonne, and Cosette finally got possession of the house. But ownership of the house came at a high price for us. Cosette's sister was opposed to the idea of us getting the house. She had always assumed that the house would be hers one day. After all, she lived in France, not us. Eventually it was arranged through the court to buy out her share in the house and other possessions. We had to assume all the expenses related to the transaction. To this was added the many types of property taxes for the house ownership, including, under French law, a tax on furnishings. After a while we realized that we could not afford two homes, one in France and one in Canada. The previous year, we sold the house after only three years of ownership.

*   *   *

Cosette's father Jaime was nineteen at the time he met his future wife in a town fair in the village. Carmen was eighteen at the time. The two soon fell in love, but Carmen's family did not approve of the young Catalan their underage daughter was dating. Jaime Palau was not liked in the village of his future bride, maybe because of the reputation of his father.

Jaime was of pudgy stock and had a short fuse to match. He had few friends that he could boast about.

The elder Mr. Mirailles forbade his daughter to continue seeing Jaime Palau, a decision that obviously displeased the young man. The couple eloped one night and travelled by train to Puigcerdà, arriving late at Jaime's aunt Pilar's door. They knocked, and although surprised, Pilar gave them shelter. Pilar ran a small inn located close to the damaged church in the center of the town. The young couple decided to stay, but to pay for their shelter they made beds, swept floors, washed the laundry, and did other menial jobs as directed by the aunt. Times were good for a while, but the civil war changed all of that.

Puigcerdà rebelled against the Franco regime, and for this the city suffered heavily under German warplanes that bombed the town, leaving behind blood and destruction. However, before the onset of the Second World War, the couple returned to France, where they were accepted back into the Mirailles clan on condition that they marry in the church and not travel to Spain in the foreseeable future. When war broke out, it was a different war, one that engulfed the whole of Europe, and Jaime was conscripted into the French army. He left his wife and two little girls in the care of the Mirailles household.

PART THREE

CHAPTER 7

August 26,2012

I received an email from my friend Anna. She wrote, "I am having an exchange with Mrs. Inserra regarding the writing of the proposed book. I also attach a copy of the letter that she has sent me... I am hopeful that you have enough time to dedicate to this project so that the work will be shared in order to achieve success."

On November 18, I met with Anna at the Inserra's residence to discuss the book, tentatively titled: *A proposal for a Book on Vancouver's Italian-Canadian Youth*.

The meeting was informal and cordial. After a light lunch of excellent lasagna and a glass of vintage Pinot Grigio, we had a roundtable discussion about the book and the division of labor. Anna suggested for the title for the book: *Breaking On the Shores of the Future: Italian Canadian Voices in Vancouver.*

The next day I began researching the subject first on the Internet, then in books I had in my library. Oddly, after researching *Italian Voices* on Wikipedia, the only names I came up with were a few names of Eastern Canada politicians. Only a handful were from Western Canada. In British Columbia the first name that popped up was Alessandro Juliani, a Canadian actor, singer, and voice actor. I had met Alessandro a few years back and seen him at the Playhouse Theater on a few occasions. Alessandro had a charming personality, but aside from his Italian roots—the son of producer, actor, and writer John Juliani—and his wonderful Italian name, I could not find any information that suggested he was a "practicing" Italian. The other was well-known singer Michael Bublé, the recipient of the Italo-Canadian man of the year award given out by the Confratellanza. Strangely, I had never heard of Bublé, as I had been out of touch with the current musical world. Next I found the name Phil Gaglardi (the proper Italian name is Gagliardi). The information gleaned on this site was inadequate, and I needed to look elsewhere.

"No, this is not the right way to search the subject," I told myself. I needed to look at other ways, other sites, and younger people. But now my mind was too preoccupied with my wife's health. How could I entertain working on such a monumental project when my wife needed me now more than ever? How could I care for her night and day?

At barely eight o'clock I found myself already exhausted and still had a pile of dishes in the sink from days before. I was already stealing a few hours from the night to extend my working days. This would require time, and time for caregiving was at a prime. So for the moment I shelved the idea and moved on to more pressing matters. However, this left me with anger at my inability to do more on Mrs. Inserra's book.

After a few weeks I was still debating the project. Would I have the time and the stamina to dedicate to the writing of anything of value that would impact the project?

Must I give it another try? I had promised Anna that I would cooperate to bring the project to fruition. Despite all other engagements, personal and otherwise, I had to find the time and energy to set my imprint on a laudable effort as planned initially.

On November 21, 2012, I was scheduled to have a biopsy for prostate cancer. I rose early and had nothing to eat or drink. I kissed Cosette at 7:00 a.m. and called for a cab to pick me up at my home for the ride to Lions Gate Hospital. When I arrived at the counter, I asked the clerk in charge where I should go for the procedure. The clerk directed me to the second-floor office. Only then was I told to go back to the lower floor.

"You can take the stairs," she advised. "The lift is being serviced today."

And so down I went again. Veering left and right through the maze of corridors, I found the place I was supposed to be adjacent to the x-ray area. I sat down in the waiting area. By this time it was 7:40 a.m. by my watch.

Seeing me pacing the floor, a clerk appeared from behind a glassed partition and announced, "We don't open until 8:00 a.m. you know. Take a seat and make yourself comfortable."

I sat down uncomfortably on a vinyl-covered chair while other patients streamed in. As I sat there, I observed the others sitting on my left and right. An elderly couple sat on my right; on my left, a man in his thirties kept playing with his car keys. In a far corner a young woman in a black coat was looking at a magazine. At exactly 8:00 a.m., the glass doors to the operating waiting area opened. There was a rush to be first. I lined up with the others, even though I had been the first one to arrive. With paper in hand—a list containing a number of questions relating to the surgery—I waited and I worried, because I had left Cosette alone in the house with the radio and the TV on.

The list read "Instructions for Prostate Surgery." The note was dated October 18th, 2012, the day after I had a scheduled appointment with the dental implant specialist and three days after Cosette had been taken to emergency in the same hospital. On the 20th, my car experienced unexpected electronic problems. I had telephoned the Honda service department and a visit was scheduled for the 22nd, the same day Cosette and I were to visit our family dentist. The car was serviced on the morning of the 23rd, leaving a small window for repairs and our departure for Hawaii.

Prior to my prostate biopsy, I had to have two fleet enemas and an antibiotic prescription filled. On the 20th, I searched for the note I had been given on the 18th and discovered that the prescription had not been filled. I rushed to the pharmacy. I was told the prescription would be ready for pickup in one hour. After picking up the prescription for four tablets of Ciproxl 100mg, I had set it aside, falsely thinking that the prescription was for painkillers and not antibiotics. I had lots of painkillers in my medicine cabinet, so why bother buying more?

I had thought wrong. On the morning of the 21ˢᵗ, when I was asked if I had taken the tablet the day before, I responded in the affirmative. I was led by a young attendant to a cubicle to undress. I put on a blue robe and walked to the biopsy room, where the nurse in attendance asked me again if I had taken the antibiotics. I made a casual comment about the painkillers being too strong.

"What painkillers are you talking about?" asked the nurse, baffled. Then she really blasted me, growling, "Mr. Rocca, we cannot proceed with the biopsy if you have not taken the antibiotic! The danger of infection is too great. I will have to consult with the doctor to see if we are to proceed, but I doubt it. Wait here and we will see."

When the nurse returned minutes later, she asked me to follow her to the I.V. room. I obliged and meekly followed her.

"We are going to give enough antibiotic. Now lie down while I hook you up to the I.V."

The procedure lasted less than half an hour, enough time for the antibiotic to be absorbed into my bloodstream. While lying down on the cot, I kept staring at the drip-drip coming down the plastic tube. Momentarily I thought about the future. I felt my life slowly draining out of me, but

I was not afraid of death. However, I was afraid of what the future held for Cosette should some unpredictable occurrence happen to me. I would not be able to care for my wife. She needed me. I needed to be healthy and strong. Forgetting things was not a good sign. But I worried, and I had to be intuitive and emphatic about it all.

How could I have made such a blunder? Was I too suffering from accelerated forgetfulness? The word "antibiotic" was spelled out three times in the notes I had with me, and I had still failed to read the note correctly. Could my faulty thinking have been the result of the stress I had been under? Had that impaired my attention? An infection could have occurred, with dire consequences. However, the biopsy was carried out without any further ado. And it is due to the attending nurse's diligence that the oversight was caught. "As we travel this road together," I kept reminding myself over and over, "I must stay strong in faith and never lose compassion for my wife, no matter what happens to me."

As a measure of this commitment, I would do whatever was required to tend to my wife's needs. But I could not control the inner turmoil going on in Cosette's mind. I was powerless to deal with her sudden swings in mood. Aside from her blindness, she had other afflictions that had imbued her life: the unspoken loneliness she felt inside, her dark world, her love for her estranged sister that was never reciprocated. I theorized all this but could never unlock it. Nor could I learn more about my wife's young life. It seemed that it was a curse, one from her paternal grandfather.

Then there was the failure of our daughter's marriage, which soured even before it began. For all of that Cosette suffered immensely. Our daughter's wedding went ahead. Martha wore her mother's wedding dress. She looked radiant despite what followed. From the very beginning, our future son-in-law insisted that everything go according to his plans. The honor guard from the Knights of Columbus, of which he was a member, had to appear at church and at the reception. The tacky affair, with hats bearing feathers and swords held high to form an arch under which the bride and the groom walked holding hands, was totally out of sync with our Italian and French tradition. Nevertheless, Martha went along with the charade. The outcome would be a somber affair nevertheless. Few of her future husband's family came to the reception. The marriage proved to be an acrimonious union that terminated in divorce, which continued in the courts at a horrible cost and mental stress. Cosette's string of bad luck would continue, unrelenting.

Sitting across from each other over dinner one evening, Cosette surprised me when she asked quizzically, "You are getting old, aren't you?"

Amused, I replied, "What makes you think that?"

She replied, "Your voice—you sound old. Your hands are not as smooth as they used to be when I touch them. And you are not patient with me. You don't like me anymore."

I was dumbfounded. I did not know what to say. I knew that in her state of mind Cosette would say odd things. I felt hurt, but knowing of her insidious malady, I kept quiet. I moved over to her and held her hand, whispering, "You know how I care for you…," and then I choked. I could not think what else to say to my poor wife.

I moved to the kitchen and started making coffee by measuring the required scoops and poured them into the coffeemaker. I turned the machine on and, addressing Cosette, who was still sitting on the sofa in the living room, I asked, "How many lumps of sugar, dear?"

"One. Only one. You know I don't take much sugar."

To change the subject I asked, "What's next on the agenda for today?"

"What agenda? You do everything. You organize all, so why ask me?"

"Sorry, I was just trying to involve you in things I do for you. Just talk, that's all."

"You never let me do anything. Sometimes you treat me as if were a screwed-up-fruitcake."

Now she was cross at me. I turned the machine on and watched the coffee pouring drip by drip into the pot. Strangely, it reminded me of the I.V. dripping life into her veins when she was in the hospital, when I did not know if she was going to make it.

"Would you like to have priest visit your wife?" the nurse had asked.

I had sighed. "A priest? Yes a priest. Today is Sunday. We both take communion on Sundays, but at this time we can't go to church to receive it."

The hospital staff had suggested a priest, because they thought Cosette was not going to pull through.

The Extreme Unction came to mind. That's when they call a priest—when you are on your last leg. Suddenly I felt a a lump in my throat. I served her coffee.

"Despite your many shortcomings, dear, you still make a good cup of coffee," she complimented me with a benign smirk on her face.

"OK, now you can drive us to the park and put me on that new wheelchair you just bought me."

I climbed down the stairs with Cosette holding onto the new railing we had installed recently. She climbed down very slowly, pausing at every step. I guided her into the car. She placed one hand on the open door, the other above on the door opening. She was having difficulty placing her left leg inside. I intervened to aid her.

"There you go again rushing me. Give me time— I'll make it. She did, and off we went, wheeling along the Seawalk in her new wheelchair. But we never went past the place where she had fainted before.

*   *   *

The pool in our backyard was used extensively during late spring, summer, and early fall. The pool lay in full view of the kitchen and dining room windows. While at home, aside from gardening, my other favorite pastime was swimming. You could see me diving and swimming lengths especially during the late afternoon, when the water temperature was at its peak. I swam alone, except when our grandchildren came to visit. I looked after the upkeep of the pool with proper chemical balancing of the water and did the vacuuming. My backyard, with many shrubs and flowers of all kinds, combined with the sparkling pool water and had reflected the happiness of our household for many years. But lately, when I looked at Cosette, I saw our happiness sucked away like the water in the skimmer of our pool.

CHAPTER 8

Ah, Paris. Cosette wished to visit Paris once more. The city of lights, the voice of the Seine, and the song of the little sparrow were calling.

"I want to visit Paris in the spring and ride the Metro and the fast trains to the Midi. I must touch the budding vines, smell the lavender of Province, walk on the pebbles, and dip my toes in the waters of Nice's Cote D'Azur, where we fell in love."

Although puzzling, this sudden wish surprised me. Cosette had sworn to never go back to France. Too many happy-sad memories crowded her mind, and she had been confused as to whether to keep them or let them go. At one time I wondered if Cosette had regretted marrying me and immigrating to Canada. Only six months earlier we had sold our house in France and had no place to stay.

Without hesitation, on the 8th of December I wrote an email to Cosette's cousins in Paris.

Dear cousins,

Cosette has decided to travel to France one more time and to visit Paris. Afterwards, we will travel by train. Our plans are to spend a week in Paris and then travel by train to the south to visit Aunt Alice in the Corbieres. Cosette would like to undertake such a voyage in the spring next year before her health takes a turn for the worst. Would it be possible for you to accommodate us for a few days?

The first response I got was over-whelming from the Paris suburbs.

It is our great pleasure to host you. You will stay with us and perhaps with your cousin Mimi in Paris as well. If Cosette is not in great form, what is her problem exactly? We need to know.

Marise

(Wife of Francis, Cosette's paternal cousin)

The second response was from St. Michel/Orge near Paris:

It is a pleasure indeed to have you with us—all the time you want. Let us know the exact time and date of your arrival. We will come get you at the airport.

Mimi

(Mimi, Francis's sister and Cosette's first godchild)

When I related the responses to my wife, she was elated.

"And I wish to visit the region of Provence and smell the lavender in bloom in Camargue when we travel to the Languedoc after Paris," Cosette uttered with elation.

Elation is a feeling my wife had been lacking lately, and had not felt since her last visit to France. For some unknown reason, she had become apprehensive about her country, the people there, and their way of life. But apprehension about what? Could the motive have been her mother's passing and the sudden break with her beloved place of birth? One day, with heavy heart, she had announced, "I'd hate to go back to France. There is nothing left there for me." Suddenly and regrettably, she felt alienated. "I didn't want the house anyway."

There was no more magical chord holding her to her native land. She felt alone and detached, cut off. Whereas for years I had felt an affinity of language and culture with my wife's land, and was entirely content with the many visits there and the house that came with it. So I rejoiced at the sudden change of heart. But before we could entertain the physical voyage, we needed to see the doctor in charge of the geriatric department, Dr. Komo. The follow-up visit with Dr. Komo would take place on December 20, 2012 at 9:30 in the morning. At first Cosette was unsure about going to see the doctor. She maintained that there was nothing wrong with her.

"What is the point in going to see doctors again and again when they cannot tell what is wrong with me?" she cried out.

Yes, the point. She had a point. Nevertheless, on the stated date we would show up at Dr. Komo's office for more information.

Cosette had always been a keen dresser. When young, she would dress in good taste, always careful with prices—a quality that impressed me. Even during our married life, her wardrobe would pass the same critical test. On the morning of the visit to the doctor, she asked me to fetch her garment from her closet—the same red gown and jacket she wore the night we dined at Chez Michel. When I handed her the suit, she did not want it. She had changed her mind. Now she wanted the blue dress.

"The long dress that our daughter Charlene gave me… that was years ago."

"It is cold out there, dear. You better wear the red one; it's a woolen one and it suits you just fine," I tried to cajole her.

"Don't tell me what I should wear," Cosette protested.

"Do you remember? The red suit is the one you got complimented on at the restaurant. They all loved it."

It took some time, but eventually she agreed to wear the red dress. But now she insisted on turning in fully dressed in her gym suit. Despondently she had said, "I feel cold. It's always too cold in this house," while I only wore a T-shirt.

Lately her hands were often icy cold, but not because of lack of comfort in the house, where the thermostat was kept at a comfortable level. But before Cosette could see Dr. Komo, I had an appointment with Dr. R. Chow at the prostate clinic to be informed about the biopsy results. The results were not too encouraging. It showed that it was cancerous, but not life-threatening. I took the news in a grouchy fashion. The doctor suggested that I undergo a bone scan to determine any more serious complications. The bone scan, scheduled for the following Wednesday morning on December 13th, would provide images of the skeleton to investigate whether the prostate cancer had spread to the bone. Dismissing all serious implications, I agreed to have the tests done. At this time I needed not concern Cosette with my own problems. Nevertheless, I was handed half a dozen booklets to read. In reading the booklets, I learned the detailed procedure of the scan and how to prepare for it mentally. This was not the news I wanted to hear, not at this moment when Cosette needed me night and day.

From the booklet titled "Just Diagnosed: (8) a guide for men and loved ones," I read the following:

Active surveillance—Is it for me?

If your cancer is unlikely to threaten your heath during your lifetime, it might be.

Perhaps your life expectancy is less than ten years, and your cancer is non-aggressive.

Perhaps all tests indicate that the cancer is slow growing and will not escape the prostate or cause symptoms.

Perhaps you have other health problems that make aggressive treatments an inferior option. Or perhaps you may decide that, given the anticipated low risk currently, you are not ready to undergo the treatment and can cope with the knowledge that cancer remains in your body.

Life for me was now suddenly reduced to a chorus of "Perhaps."

Perhaps I will live or I will die.

Perhaps I will be able to care for my sick wife.

Perhaps she will get better.

Perhaps I will require help to support myself.

Perhaps I will be shocked, worried, scared, or anxious.

Perhaps I will feel angry and lonely, or perhaps I will be sad or feel hopeless.

Perhaps I will shout in poetic form.

I would turn into Hamlet and, holding a skull in my hands, I'd recite one more time: "To be or not to be. That is the question."

The booklet continued its advice: "In the final analysis, no one can tell any individual patient who has prostate cancer exactly how he will fare. Unfortunately, doctors do not yet have a 'crystal ball' to predict tumor behavior. Neither are they 'the purveyors of magic and miracles.'"

I had many feelings, but I refused to feel hopeless.

"Marc," my wife called out, "I need to go to the bathroom!"

"Yes, dear, I will be right up."

My appointment at the hospital's Nuclear Medicine Department for the nuclear bone scan was at 8:30 a.m. Lying on a cot, I was injected with a small amount of radioactive material in a vein in my right arm. From there, over a few hours, it would collect in areas of the skeleton where there were metastatic (abnormal)(5) cancer cells. If "hot spots" were detected by a gamma camera, then an x-ray would be taken to confirm the diagnosis that cancer did exist there. I returned two hours later to be escorted into the room where the gamma camera was located.

The prostate specific antigen (PSA) readings had begun to show above-normal levels in my system. My next visit to Dr. Chow was scheduled for January 21, 2013.

*   *   *

A week later, on December 20 at 9:30 a.m., we were both back for an appointment.

The visit to the specialist in Geriatric Medicine did not reveal anything out of the ordinary, only confirming what I had always suspected about Cosette's level of incapacity and the reactions to some of the medication she was taking. The in-home care issue was discussed with Cosette who, for the moment, was adamant about not having anyone in the house looking after her—except her husband, of course. Dr. Komo wrote a report to our family doctor:

DEMENTIA

She does have dementia. It makes it hard because she is quite anxious and she is blind. She was started on Exelon patch 5 and did okay besides skin irritation, and then went up to patch 10 just as she was being discharged from the outreach program. Now she complains of GI side effects. Her husband says that she is clinically pretty stable besides her irritability. Considering everything, we will have to make a change.

PLAN

We will stop Exelon (she wants to finish out her prescription), and then we will start her on Reminyl, hoping that she tolerates it from a GI perspective. If she does not, maybe we will try her on Ebixa.

ANXIETY

Anxiety continues to be an issue. Her sleep is not perfect, but we do not expect it to be. She is, however, more anxious in general. It is hard to discern how much of this is baseline anxiety, how much is her personality, and how much of this is her and her husband just not really getting along with the situation at home. Things seem to be pretty difficult though.

PLAN
I have increased her Remeron from 1 to 1-1/2 of a 15 mg tablet a night and will see how she does.

*   *   *

This is the note that I was given by Dr. Komo:

Points that need to be addressed:

1. Finish the Exelon Patch, then wait one week
2. Fill out new prescriptions and start after being off Exelon for one week
3. Look into Lifeline
4. I'll call in an increase to the night pill (for better sleep and less anxiety)
5. I'll see you in three months' time

It was obvious that, at the stage Cosette found herself, she could not make subjective decisions. The doctor should have overruled her and suggested instead that the matter be left in the hands of her caregiver. After discussing the in-home care issue in some detail, and Cosette's opposition to it, the arrangements were not discussed any further. Thereafter, irked, Dr. Komo rose from his chair, declaring, "You can squabble that between the two of you," and left the room. The term "squabble" was offensive to me. When I looked up the meaning of the word in my *Webster's Dictionary* I found it meant to: "engage in noisy but not very serious argument," and I was put off.

Is this what Dr. Komo meant when he wrote in the report: *she and her husband just not really getting along with the situation at home?* Could this be one of the reasons Cosette disliked the doctor?

So much for the medical profession, I thought. In the end, if the doctor was irked, so were we. We did not like the way we were dismissed by the health care specialist one bit. I had tried to engage the doctor to be more proactive in the matter of in-home care with Cosette, but my attempts resulted in being slighted by the doctor. Why is it that when we needed more support from health professionals who are paid from public funds that we were accused of squabbling?

"We want to see a neurologist." This is the question I asked our family doctor, Dr. Smith.

Dr. Komo had identified the caregiver burden as being an issue. Clearly, aside from the cleaning woman who came twice a month on Thursdays, Cosette had no intention of having another stranger in the house to help with daily chores. The fact of the matter was that she needed help, I needed help, and the household could do with the presence of an extra person looking after Cosette. I could not do it alone. But every time the subject was broached another war broke out, new battles and new threats reverberating in the halls of the house. So when I pursued the matter, it would result in another bridge-jumping threat.

"You are not going to do this to me. I'll move to another room! I'll move out! I will… you know me, when I get upset, I can't think."

All of this—our senior home arrangements—I wished to discuss with Dr. Komo.

But the doctor was in a hurry because of other arrangements. If, when, and where would Cosette be placed should she become unmanageable? These were my questions. Yet I was informed that they could wait until the next visit three months hence!

"In any case, things won't get any worse for another 2-3 years," he had said.

But suppose that her situation got worse earlier, then what? Hadn't they told me that I needed to prepare myself for all eventualities? How could I plan for the future—find a place, place Cosette on a waiting list, and then wait for things to happen?

Look into Lifeline for your wife. That way she can call for help instantly. The doctor had marked this on his pad.

In objecting to having more help at home, Cosette had revisited her jealousy closet. Was it a zealous desire to preserve the existing situation based on her desire to retain a modicum of independence that drove her to deny herself additional help? To do nothing and not give me extra time to be by myself once in a while? Jealousy is based on lack of trust. Cosette could never have any reason to be jealous of her husband of many years. Or had she a buried desire to be like her mother, who was deeply jealous of everyone and everything? Cosette was now jealous me. Bouts of jealousy that were just under the skin would surface in fits whenever I had to meet with old female friends for one reason or another. Cosette would be insufferable when this happened.

"You want another person in the house looking after me so that you can be free to leave the house and do what pleases you."

The battle went on and on. The bottle caps flew open. Tiny pills dropped into my hand and bigger glasses were raised high more frequently than before to drown the pain.

Finally, on December 20 at 4:50 p.m., our visit to the family doctor took place. Both Cosette and I took turns being asked questions. But first it started with her blood pressure, which was slightly above normal at the time. Then Dr. Smith asked my wife how she was faring at home and whether she had home care help.

My wife renewed her opposition to hire any help to aid her at home. Realizing that she would not budge on the subject, the doctor asked that Cosette be escorted out of the office so that he could talk to me privately. Being aware of the dire situation in our home, the doctor laid it out quite clearly. It was up to me to see that we got home care help and soon. Now I could be happier, and I was relieved to have the doctor backing me up for a change. Now I could go ahead with hiring home care support.

CHAPTER 9

Cosette had been behind many a decision affecting our lives. She was part and parcel of my life. Now one part of my life was broken, and I could not fix it. I found myself alone. Alone to make decisions without her beside me. In the past, I would sometimes do things the wrong way to get them right. I was faced with the possibility that things would not work out at all. Things had changed, and I was afraid.

I was well aware that, on some days, living with Cosette was more stressful than other days. Now I saw myself in a gilded cage, and no longer could I hear the birdsong of my partner. The cage that life had thrust on us had become a leaden casing. One night, after watching Cosette's preferred

TV program on AMI, she asked for a glass of water. I went into the kitchen, poured only half a glass, and gave it to my wife with the prescribed nightly medication.

"It's too darn cold!" she protested. "Go fetch me another, and this time bring it to me lukewarm."

Afterwards, when entering the bed with her gym suit on and in an agitated state, Cosette moved the pillow to the bed. "You are always moving things for me," she commented, annoyed. "Two beds are supposed to be here, not one!"

Moving things had become a statement that repeated itself many times, and the way she interpreted things, they were always on the move. Was this outburst an act of subconscious separation?

"No, dearie," I corrected her. "Only one bed—our bed. We have a queen-sized bed. We have always slept in one bed, never two. Please place the pillow back the way it was. It will be easier for you to sleep with your head on the pillow next to mine. That way we can be face-to-face and feel each other's breath, and your pajamas…."

But before I could finish the sentence, Cosette sneered at me. "Don't you 'dearie' me. I am quite capable of looking after myself."

I insisted; she persisted. We fought, and in the end she had her own way. Had she lost her sense of humor? After we turned in, she spent the next half-hour fussing about and talking, not making any sense. Sleep did not come easy to me that night. Strangely, despite Cosette's outbursts, I dreamed about making love to my wife that night. I still loved her; I still desired her. But I worried. I worried that if her behavior should worsen, it would cast doubts on the future of our life together.

Often she didn't know her husband anymore. I was a total stranger to her. And I had to accept the reality that we would be living together as strangers. Perhaps that way it would be less painful for me. Then I remembered a line in the movie *Trouble in Paradise* that we had recently watched: "Marriage is a beautiful mistake that people make together." Real love doesn't exist, or does it? But then how does dementia affect love, real or not?

In the great wheel of human solitude and responsibility, I knew I represented a small cog among the suffering multitude. I realized that, as a person on this earth, I had to bear my share to achieve my unique life. But regrets began entering my mind. Perhaps my pursuit of happiness had been a fake wish. It started with doubts about Cosette's subconscious sincerity. For all I knew, she had not loved me at all. She married me to get away from her parents because she had not been happy with them back in France. Meeting me on the beach in France was an escape, allowing for her to leave them behind and with them her unhappy childhood. Cosette never spoke about her youth. Did she ever fall in love before she met me? Was she attracted to boys? Was I the first boy she kissed? Did she ever have sex before she met me?

She might not have had a stable childhood to begin with. Her parents kept moving from one place to another, especially after her father's transfer to Ludwigshaffen in occupied West Germany soon after the war. She spent the next four years there, going to French schools and never being allowed outdoors to have fun with German children or get to know them. The only times she was allowed to visit Mannheim across the river was with her French-speaking German maid, Emma Ronstad. Cosette had outgrown her sister in everything but her sibling's desire to go out chasing boys. But her sister had become unruly and promiscuous with a G.I. in the nearby base.

"My sister was a *putte*... you know what."

I didn't need Cosette to tell me more. Because of her sister's debauched behavior, her father requested a transfer, this time in Bar-le-duc and later Revigny. It was a smaller town, but not far away enough for her sister's wild escapades. She was in her late teens when her father was finally posted to St. Martin, a mountain village in the French Alps. This is when

I met her on the beach in Villefranche, next door to Nice.

A flower had bloomed on the pebbles of a French beach long ago. Now the flower was in my hands, wilting before my eyes.

*   *   *

On December 14, 2012, Cosette felt grief when the news reported the horrible slaughter of children that had taken place in the Sandy Hook School in Newtown, Connecticut. What was another handicap for her in the face of the grief of the many fathers and mothers losing their children to a demented act of savagery? What was human suffering, and how did Cosette and I measure humans' acts of folly against natural occurrences of illness of the human body? Cosette felt a cry inside her, but a human cry, lost in a world of incomprehension. "Why are we destroying one another?" she asked.

What does anyone feel when we look at ourselves in the mirror, pointing a gun? What is the culture of gun ownership that only serves to kill? Looking confused, I would look heavenward for answers. Would it help to fall down on my knees? Would this simple act of faith console the parents of those children?

The next days would prove more challenging. While Cosette's battle raged furiously on one front, there was a truce on the other—my prostate problems.

It all hung on what Dr. Komo had to say about Cosette, I kept telling myself. In the meantime, the initial report on my bone scan was not so ominous as to lose more sleep over it. Nonetheless, I still required more visits with Dr. V Chow, the doctor in charge of my prostate cancer for the next few weeks, to review the official results of the nuclear scan.

The results were negative, so no bone cancer. Dr. Chow put me on new medication:

Dutaster/Tamsulo 0.5/0. 4mg

This medication is typically used to relieve the symptoms of benign prostatic hyperplasia (BPH)

Possible side effects.

It may lower your sex drive (libido), and it can affect ejaculation. It may cause difficulty with erection. Occasionally, it may cause breast development in men, and it may cause breasts to feel swollen and tender.

Each person may react differently to a treatment. If you think this medication may be causing side effects (including

*those described here or others), talk to
your doctor or pharmacist.*

There you have it. Soon I would be caressing my own breasts instead of caressing myself elsewhere. But would I be able to have a normal flow when peeing? The way I saw it, at my age I worried more about pissing normally than anything else. I brought these concerns to my family doctor. I told him that I did not fancy growing breasts and that I wished to stop taking the medication.

Soon Dr. Smith advised me, "It's your choice if you don't want to take it, but you also have refused radiation and other intrusive treatments. To arrest the cancer I suggest that you take the Duster/ Tamsulo as suggested by Dr. Chow."

June 2010: the month of new discoveries.

In all of the recent occurrences at home, I seldom thought about my native country: Italy. The last time I asked Cosette to travel with me was to attend the 13th Biennial Conference in June 2010, organized by the AICW (Association of Italian Canadian Writers). It had been a memorable event for me to participate in as a contributing writer. The theme of the conference had been aptly chosen. "Writing Our Way Home" (10) grew out of the academic and literary presentation delivered during the 13th biennial conference of the AICW held in Atri on June 10-13, 2010 at Hotel Du Parc, Atri (Teramo),

Italy. But before we returned home, I wished to visit the region of Abruzzo, where a terrible earthquake had recently devastated the area of L'Aquila and the surrounding villages. We had left Vancouver on the 1st of June, renting a car at the airport in Toulouse and spending the first two days with friends at Gargas, a farming village just outside the pink city (Toulouse la ville Rose). Next, after spending four days in their house in the Corbieres, we took the road again, making stops in Menton on the Baie Du Soleil, where Cosette caught up with her old friend Michelle. Crossing into Italy via Autoroute A9 and A8, and then Autostrada A7, we spent one night in Bologna to visit Esterina, my old friend from my native village. We arrived in Atri for the conference, scheduled to take place at the Du Parc Hotel during the next three days. The conference had been a resounding success. I met with many writers of Italian origin, many of them accomplished in their own fields of writing.

After the conference and during the next two weeks, we toured the southern part of Italy, visiting friends and family in Basilicata and Abruzzo. My dear maternal uncle Pietro was still alive then. While in my hometown, I visited my childhood stomping grounds, reliving part of his past. But now my dear wife was by my side. Though dear to me, I never really regretted leaving my place of birth, which had been so badly ravaged by the war. The memory of my childhood and early youth were filled with disappointments and betrayals.

But then home called us back to Vancouver to our daughters and granddaughters. Returning to France via Tuscany, where we occupied ourselves by revisiting my maternal cousin Cesco and the treasure that is Florence, we felt on top of the art world. We proceeded westward along the historically rich and dynamic region of Liguria. Here, mountains and cliffs rise loftily out of the sea and offered a fascinating landscape to the traveler. I looked for a hotel to spend the night. The next day, before entering into France through Menton, I planned to visit the beaches of the Italian Riviera, where tourists have been flocking for ages, and experience the great seafood that the region had to offer.

We rose early with the charm of the deep blue water and with the sun on our backs. We were once again in the splendid vineyard of Languedoc-Roussillon. Finally, returning to Cosette's aunt's place, we were welcomed again with open arms by her mother's sister Alice, a most jovial and generous person. She was welcoming and hospitable. Alice had all the positive human qualities that her older sister lacked.

"You should have been my mother," Cosette once told her aunt.

Without any hesitation, Auntie Alice, who only had two sons, replied, "And you, Cosette, should have been my daughter." They had hugged warmly.

In Gargas, a town twenty kilometres outside of Toulouse, in the garden of our friend Christiane Puges, I picked the tastiest persimmons from a tree growing just outside the guest bedroom window. While guests in the farmhouse, Cosette and I were treated to a generous hospitality that only country people could offer. We enjoyed the walks along country roads amid vast fields of soybeans, sunflowers, and wheat that our friends cultivated. We felt accomplished and, aside from Cosette's visual impairment, we laughed and were happy.

Later at home, while looking at photographs of our voyage, I would laugh at the sight of myself trying to ride a donkey in the square of my hometown, only to be thrown off its saddle to the villagers' amusement. Or remembering the trick that our friend Jean Puges had played on me while hunting in the fields around Gargas. When I was shown a rabbit, I took aim and fired. A puff of dust rose from the shot rabbit. Jean had filled a decoy with sawdust and cinder to fool me. What a laugh that was. All was in good humor.

I worried about the prostate that was deep in my pelvis and surrounded the urethra as it left the bladder. Three weeks after the scan I noticed a dark mix I had never seen before. The doctor told me that there might be some blood in the urine after the scan, but he had not mentioned anything about blood in the semen. I felt tired and lacked energy. These feelings of fatigue were different than normal feelings of being tired. Again life for me seemed less secure and predictable. Perhaps now was the time to talk with my doctor to see whether anti-anxiety medication would be helpful. I hoped that the predicament I found myself in would not be stressful or upsetting enough to see a doctor. But times had changed. There was little laughter in the home that had seen so much happiness in our life together. I withdrew socially. Stress started to take its toll. I felt anxiety and suffered from sleeplessness, waking up exhausted and irritable. Fatigue set in. In the face of all this, I was reminded to be calm. I wished to be free, the kind of freedom that writing could offer, when my mind could wander the universe and find humanity in the stars, but with my feet still planted on Earth. One option I saw looming ahead was to get professional in-home care services to help in the household and personal care of my wife.

In the meantime, to keep my mind busy I resumed writing short stories and articles for the local Italian newspaper. When lack of sleep kept me tossing in bed, I got up to watch TV while my wife slept. But even that did not satisfy my restlessness. Strangely, after I resumed writing, my clearest thoughts came to me in the darkness and solitude of night. The result of this work showed up in the stories I wrote.

Seven Wolves, a fictional story about my grandfather's encounter with wolves one winter long ago, was written during that time. So was *The Crown of Pearls*, another fictional story about two old cronies talking about the virtue of giving and being upstanding members of the community. As was an article titled "The Internment of Italian-Canadians." Not that these works had much literary value, but they offered me a temporary alternative to keep my mind clear from constant worrying about Cosette. The ache of grief was always there that my wife's conditions would get worse. I knew that eventually she needed to be placed in a suitable care facility.

From Dr.Komo's report I read: "He also wonders about maybe getting her name on a waitlist for the Italian care home that he has (selected) across town, and we talked a little bit about how she needs a long term care assessment, and she would have to get a bed on the North shore."

The Villa Carital care home facility at the Italian Centre was moved forward from the backburner. However, I was advised that the wait there was between 18-24 months—that's how difficult it was to wait for a nursing home. Perhaps what I needed was some other form of distraction. I had given myself a structure and purpose in life. I believed in the sanctity of marriage, I had worked much of my adult life for the same company, I had lived in the same house for what seemed an eternity (and I hoped it stayed so). To keep fit, I had played badminton twice weekly for twenty-five years, and when that stopped I took up running and, later on, lawn bowling.

What was it that now made the rivets of my armor begin popping out with more frequency? My awareness that Cosette had rejected all sorts of niceties, and worst of all, had lost interest in my advances (sexual or otherwise), put a definite chill in our relationship. She had become bone-dry in body and in spirit. And when hot flashes inflamed her body, her hands turned into the tips of icebergs. But what could I do when abdominal pains, signs of internal psychological turmoil, began gnawing away at my insides and chewing my brains out? How did other people deal with all the pain they had to endure? Would alcohol, painkillers, or even Lorazepam calm my nerves and soothe my anxious soul? Over the span of our lives, it seemed that Cosette had imprisoned me to the point of being oppressive. To be in love with someone and then discover that love reciprocated was a jealousy of the heart was no longer pure and therefore was questionable. "Go ahead. Get yourself another woman!" she shouted at me, full of jealousy.

PART FOUR

CHAPTER 10

In life, some people have few wishes. Others have many: wishes to own, to choose where to live and where to die, whom to marry, what friends to have, and where to travel, among others. In better days, Cosette loved horses and flamingos, and she always had a wish to visit a region of her country of birth where both abounded in the wild. Cosette and I had done our fair share of travelling. Being originally from France and Italy, we visited our home countries quite often. In addition, we toured Southern Spain's Catalunia as well as visiting southern Europe from the Alps to the Atlantic. We traveled to and loved Australia, in particular the East Coast. In the Mexican Riviera, we spent many weeks both in the spring and in the winter on the Pacific Coast. We visited Florida and took cruises to the Caribbean Islands many times. But there was an area Cosette wished to visit most of all: the Camargue, the region south of Arles in France and between the Mediterranean Sea and the Rhone River delta.

"I want to see the white horses of Camargue when we go to France next spring."

This was a vast expanse of marshy plain that was designated as a Wetland of International Importance in 1986. In past voyages, much to Cosette's chagrin and my need to move on, I often drove past this area on out way to the Cote d'Azure and Italy, but never stopped by to visit. I promised my wife that the next voyage to France would include a visit to Les Saintes Maries de La Mere at the tip of the Camargue. However, this was a dream that would be shattered before our flight began.

CHAPTER 11

What lifts my spirits from time to time are instances when Cosette displays her remarkable self in a surprising way. I still love my wife for it.

"Marc, do I have emotions sometimes?"

Certainly that was a change of thinking. "Emotions you have plenty of, my dear. You cry, you are angry, you shout, you are restless, you feel dejected and have regrets. I am sure you feel love but do not know how to express it in words or actions, and mostly you get frustrated. But you must not feel unloved. Our children and grandchildren love you, and I love you."

"Marc, can I change?" she pleaded. Then the mood changed as swiftly as a blast of wind chasing away the gray sky.

"Can I say that my name is Dementia? It sounds nice, like a girl's name," she laughed. "In this hotel nobody knows my real name." She thought we were staying in a hotel. "Sometimes I forget we are in Vancouver. We have been here before, haven't we?"

"Yes dear, we come here often," I reassured her. "We'll come back here anytime you want."

Going back to the subject of changing, I told her, "We cannot change what is unchangeable. We'll try to do our best, dear Dementia."

I laughed too. She hadn't had a good hearty laugh for quite a while, and I welcomed her unusual levity. But were moments like these enough to encourage me to go on? What was my duty to my wife?

Patience, my dear… is a virtue few people have and the envy of many. So, my dear… remember to be patient and people will admire you. …I know of only one duty, and that is to love… and where there is no hope, it is incumbent on us to invent it."

–Albert Camus.

I was lost and I needed to find myself.

In one dream, I saw myself stark naked and lost in a mansion in a vast estate. I searched many rooms. I found them all empty. Then I saw someone of importance—a keeper of sorts. "How can I get back to my wife? Please show me the road," I asked.

The keeper told me to spend a couple of nights at the inn, told me to have some dinner, and then he would show me the road. I had no intention of staying two nights at the inn, and I was not hungry. Anyway, I had no money to pay for the food and the room. I was naked, so how could I pay for anything? I just wanted to go home to my wife. I looked for a sign, and as I walked around with my head and hands held low, I felt ashamed and fragile. No one could help me. I needed to empty myself.

Cosette's pleading jarred me awake.

"I can't find the washroom. Take me to the washroom!"

What was wrong with my sleep? I could not make any sense of it.

*   *   *

It was December 31, 2012. The end of the year was here. There was really nothing ordinary about it. Nevertheless, it had been a very remarkable year. It started with a bang at a gala New Year's party held at the Italian Cultural Centre. Balloons were popped and glasses tipped. Hugs and kisses for lovers and friends. A late summer sun had shone for weeks— one to remember—gold and silver everywhere. In years past, there had been plenty of sunshine in our backyard. Here, growing in a sunny corner of the garden, I had planted a fig tree, perhaps in remembrance of happy days. Every year the tree produced delicious white figs that Cosette enjoyed eating. One late summer day, I took Cosette by the hand and led her under the tree. The figs were ripe and sweet. Selecting one low-lying branch, I held it for Cosette to pick a few ripe fruits. She ate one fruit with enjoyment, then another. Later, holding my arm, she walked under the tree where dry leaves had fallen during the hot summer weather.

Surprising her, I asked, "Do you remember when we were younger, one of our visits to Spain with the fig trees by the roadside? Where you played Eve, lying naked on dry fig leaves? You decided to consecrate the moment to the happiness of our life."

"Ah, you fool. I did no such thing! You are lying. You always invent things. Take me inside," she demanded.

At times she remembered nothing, as if she did not exist, leaving me with only the memory of our life together. For me the fig tree had always symbolized life and stood for knowledge and good. I remembered from the Bible that Adam and Eve used the leaves of the fig tree to cover themselves after the fall, when they realized they were naked (Genesis 3:7). So it was very fitting to make mention of the fig tree to Cosette.

Now and then I played games with her, making her believe that she was right, that she was not home but somewhere else. As we walked into our bedroom, she thought she was in a hotel room, somewhere imagined.

"We have been here before. I remember this place," she said with confusion.

"You like coming here often, don't you?" I quizzed her, waiting for no reply.

I told her lies to aid her mistaken beliefs of being, of existing. To make her believe she was in another space, I promise to take her to a different hotel every night. I did not get angry at her confusion anymore, and that's how life went on—a life imagined. She was by my side, but with a new companion called dementia to keep us company.

For the first time in many years, Cosette and I did not celebrate the coming of the new year. For the first time, there were no colored balloons or noisemakers and no happy rattling rejoicing in our hearts. By the fireplace we sat, watching old movies on TV with Cosette just listening. Around midnight I rose to fetch a bottle of bubbly. I popped the cork and poured a full glass for myself and a half-glass for Cosette. We ate some figs and dates. At midnight I refilled my glass and poured another half-glass for Cosette. Between the old and the new year, we kissed, still taking pleasure in the delicious fruit. At

1 a.m., holding each other by the arm, we clambered up the stairs to our bedroom. The bubbly worked wonders on Cosette, allowing her a bit of levity at year's end. Before she could reach the bedroom door, she became ill. She needed to relieve herself. She was not supposed to drink any alcohol. Doing so did not agree with her medication. It was *mea culpa mea maxima culpa* for me. Damn the bubbly Prosecco! There was really nothing ordinary about the year 2012.

CHAPTER 12

In February 2013, before getting into bed one night, Cosette, visibly agitated, pronounced, "I don't like this woman in my house! There is something I don't like about her. I don't know why."

The woman was Astra, our new homemaker. She had been hired through an agency recommended by Dr.Komo's office. She came twice a week to tend to my wife for four hours each time. This arrangement gave me a chance to be away from my residence and not have to worry about leaving Cosette alone in the house. The helper's chores were: personal care, home support, and companionship for Cosette. She arrived at 12:45 p.m. and left at 4:45 p.m. Astra was

Polish but spoke a bit of Italian and had a smattering of French. I judged her to be a reasonable worker.

One day, talking about herself, Astra confided that she had spent three years in Italy. I suspected that she was referring to a refugee camp where annually hordes of poor refugees from all over the world seek shelter and protection from persecution. After a determined stay in a UN camp, the refugees were dispersed again until other countries offered them asylum.

What was it Cosette did not like? The past few weeks I had been content about the arrangement. Finally I had someone in the house, and I could take a break from my caregiving duties. But now this "I don't like" from Cosette!

This new conflict emerging in our household—brought by the presence of our hired homemaker, whose actions were both welcome and intrusive—worried me. Cosette was unable to define Astra's presence in our house. However, I think Astra was challenging my instructions about wearing appropriate footwear in the house (such as slippers or socks) and avoiding the use of foul language. She had indicated that she preferred to go barefoot, as she liked the soft feeling of the carpet under her feet. She said that it gave her a sense of freedom. To avoid the spread of germs, I never permitted my children to walk around the house with bare feet. This intention was bred in me long ago after I walked barefoot both at home and outdoors as a child but never liked it.

But there was another troubling aspect regarding Astra's behavior, one that had nothing to do with her work but with her foul language in Italian—which Cosette understood well. I presumed that habit of using swear words was picked up while in the camp in Italy. To me it was sublimely vulgar to swear to the Virgin Mary in Italian or any other language for that matter, and I did not condone it, especially in my house. I was sure the woman knew the meaning of her swearing, but she took it all too lightly. So I had to deal with her vulgar language.

I sensed that Cosette felt my dilemma and reacted oddly. However, I had determined that during the next visit I would advise Astra about her disregard for my instructions. I would dismiss her if she refused. But would this be too drastic a measure to take? Or should I compromise in dealing with this conflict? Should I face the task of having to hire another worker anew? And would that solve my wife's unexplained anxiety with this matter?

A friend suggested that we take a breather—a short trip away from home. "You both need a break," she said. "Why don't you both travel south to the US? A short visit."

When I mentioned to Cosette that I wanted to take her for a trip, she worried. She worried about the finances now, about the help we hired to clean the house and for care assistance.

"Can we afford it?" she queried.

I tried to reassure her that yes, we could afford it and not to worry.

"I worked all my life. Where is my money? You are spending all my money!"

Suddenly her mood swung. She asked practical questions. She was reasonable. "Do we need passports to go to the States?"

"Why do you ask? Of course we need passports. We're going to another country!"

"Sometimes you forget." That's all she said, smiling playfully.

Was this just an offhand statement, or did Cosette sense something about my remembering things? For a few minutes nothing else was said. She sat at the edge of the chair like she always did and scooped crumbs of bread from the table. She collected the tiny specks in her left hand until it was time to get up.

"Sometimes you forget my medication. The other day you forgot. That's all," she said, sulking and reminding me that she could not trust me. "You forget things like I do. You better go see a doctor."

For me, this was a switch. I needed to have someone look after me now. She was suggesting that I might have dementia myself. Abruptly, something bothered me about what she said. She sensed, she read me and she doubted me. How could I forget to administer her medication on time? And to forget our passports in the safety box at the bank?

You fool, I told myself. Soon we would be leaving for our trip to the States and I forgot to pack our passports! In a panic, I sprang from my chair and walked to the dresser in our bedroom. I searched the drawers but found nothing. I searched everywhere, but I came up empty-handed. I was sure I had them with me, but I could not find them. I was sure I had not taken them to the bank vault after our last trip to Hawaii.

"I need to gas up before we go. I'll be back shortly." Full of guilt, I lied. I would not confess to being so forgetful. I could not tell my wife the truth that I did not remember where I had placed our passports.

At the bank, I asked for my box. It was brought to me. I opened the box in the cubicle and thankfully, the passports were there. I removed them and placed them in my breast pocket, close to my heart.

I had booked a three-day respite to Everett in Washington State on *Booking.com.* Why did I pick Everett? Because the area appealed to me at that moment, I had never been there before, and because the price suited me. I did not mention the word casino to Cosette for fear that she would not approve. It was a reasonably balmy day when we left our home. By two thirty on the afternoon of February 8, we were at the Best Western Cascade Inn in Everett. After I checked in, I parked the car in the reserved parking spot for people with disabilities. On entering the inn, I noticed that renovations were going on.

Tired from the journey, we retired early. The first night, a Friday, was one of rest. The next day the sky was cloudy, a steady, misty rain falling. We did some touring, visiting St. Mary village, had lunch, and later stopped by the Tulalip Casino, where cigarette and cigar smoking was allowed indoors, and the noise was nonstop—one of the most polluted places in the Northwest. We returned to the inn around seven p.m. Soon afterwards, we dined at Denny's next door. By nine p.m. we were in bed sleeping.

But soon after I was awakened by noises— stomping feet, running in corridors—coming from the upper floor. Then around eleven p.m., the level of noise increased. By midnight I heard voices and bottles breaking below our window, followed by running on the roof above the lobby and below our window. By one-thirty a.m. the noise above us was still going on, and the loitering on the roof became very annoying. I finally opened the window to investigate. I saw two dark shadows prowling about on the roof and one man sitting against the wall with a bottle of beer in his hand. As I became concerned about the intrusion on the lobby roof, I called the front desk attendant and notified him regarding the fracas below our window.

"What roof? There is no roof on the second floor!" the attendant asked, incredulous. He must have been thinking I was dreaming.

"The roof over the foyer—the lobby!" I told him, refraining from swearing. Didn't he know there were windows looking onto the lobby's flat roof?

Still doubtful, he asked if he could come up to our room to investigate. When he arrived Cosette ducked under the covers, wondering what it was all about. I promptly showed the attendant the window and, pulling back the curtain, I asked him to look. Was he surprised! He slid the window open and spoke to the intruders to get off the roof terrace. One of them, drunk and foul-mouthed, told him to fuck off.

"Get off of there or I'll call the cops!" the attendant admonished them. Then, more forcefully this time, he repeated his warning: "Come down from there to my office now! I will have you thrown out!"

In the meantime, Cosette was wondering what was going on. She couldn't see all the fuss, but she could hear the commotion going on in our room and outside the window. As well, there was another kind of noise going on upstairs a noisy party.

Surely she must have asked herself these two questions: what has Marc done? Where has he taken me? She must be wondering—and worrying. I was concerned as well and trusted that the attendant could defuse the situation and bring it to an end. Still, I was concerned that things might escalate to the point where our own safety would be put into jeopardy.

We didn't need this. I blamed myself. How had I come to this?

Eventually, the rowdies were off the roof only after I threatened them to call the police myself.

Worried, the attendant begged. "No, no. Let me handle this."

But the noise in the corridors and the adjacent rooms, as well as the noise above us, continued unabated. By five a.m., I had slept hardly a wink.

The next morning Cosette urged me to speak to the management to do something about the bill. "You are not going to pay the bill, are you? This has been a waste of our money."

By eight, I was at the desk addressing the new attendant about our displeasure about what had happened during the night and the following morning. I gave notice that we would be vacating the room the same day and warning that I would take action against the hotel legally if need be, and even posting the events of that terrible night on the internet for all to know. I demanded that I be reimbursed the cost of the three nights I had already prepaid. The woman at the desk offered to refund me a paltry forty dollars. I laughed at her and requested that she contact the manager immediately to deal with the matter.

"I shall be back before nine to check out," I said and walked away with impatient steps. At the same time I was trying to guide my wife to the elevator, but she seemed to be frozen and wouldn't budge. A burning thought crossed my mind—was this the beginning of another stroke? At once I worried that she might slump to the floor. I held her close and began a slow walk toward the elevator to go pack our things. Cosette's reaction was not lost on the attendant.

When I returned, alone, to the front desk, the attendant informed me there was no word from the manager, but she was more acquiescing this time. She offered to credit one night and not charge for the next as we were checking out. The great escape from our home conflicts had ended with a night full of excitement, acrimony, and a lack of sleep. We were again on our way home and reached the Linden border crossing by three p.m.

I had taken a detour to shop at the duty-free store, mostly to drop in at on our daughter Martha, who lived in Mission not far from the US border. I stopped briefly at the White Spot on Meridian Ave. to call Martha on my cell phone. We had not been to her place since she had bought it six years ago after her divorce. Stopping at that White Spot reminded me of happier times. I would see my ex-son-in-law with my daughter and their two daughters, now torn apart and in bitterness.

Unsure of finding her home, I was surprised and pleased when I heard her voice. "Sorry Dad, I am not at home but visiting with friends," she said matter-of-factly.

"Visiting friends you say? We haven't been to your place for five years or more and you can't break off from your friends to receive us?" I was pissed off.

Cosette read me. "That's your daughter for you— the nerve! You better stop financing her. She doesn't deserve it."

The next night Cosette would feel the effects of the commotion experienced the night before at the hotel and added to it our daughter's rejection. She became agitated and incoherent again. The terror of the previous night surely affected her, as did the silent inner stab she felt after our daughter's lack of sensitivity.

However, a day later the whole affair at the hotel had a bittersweet ending from a financial point of view when I received an email from the General Manger Best Western
Cascadia Inn.

Dear Mr. Rocca,

Thank you for completing the survey regarding your recent stay at our property.

Your business is very important to us, and we value your feedback. By telling us what you liked about your stay and how we can improve, you are helping us deliver a superior experience for you and other guests in the future, I am very disappointed that other guests ruined you night at the hotel. I have credited your VISA card for your stay. Again, I apologize.

Thank you again for taking the time to complete the survey. We appreciate your loyalty to our brand.

Sincerely
K.L.

General manager,
Best Western Cascadia Inn

Because of the quick response to my complaint by the management of the largest hotel chain in the world, my faith and loyalty to the good hospitality levels in the hotel business was restored, albeit with careful consideration to future traveling.

Unfortunately, after I read the email to Cosette, the bitterness of it remained entrenched in her mind. "Next time, think about where you take me, my dear husband." Her voice had a warning tone to it. But soon her mood swung to a more condescending one when she added, "You see? Sometimes when you listen to me it does you and me good." She smiled at me craftily, but she was not finished yet when she threw another subtle warning. "Perhaps we should take a long rest from our travels."

Then, changing the subject, she asked me, "The old hand railing in the stairwell is coming apart. You better fix it and soon. You don't expect me to go tumbling down and also break my neck!" She also had other projects for me. "The inside walls of the house could do with some fresh paint!"

This is what I thought of my blind and clever wife who had some sort of dementia: "Yes, Cosette, despite all, you have kept your spirit and you are still wonderful! But to replace the hand rail and paint the walls again? No, I think I'll hire a painter and a carpenter to do it. For the moment I will retire to my sofa instead and look back at our wonderful, sweet, and yes, at times sour moments we had together, especially when we were younger and full of dreams."

PART FIVE

CHAPTER 13

COME WALK WITH ME COSETTE

Here are my wife's flitting memories. Time and space fluctuate back and forth; she needs to tell me her side of the story.

*   *   *

Like a knitted sweater, my life is coming undone bit by bit, pulled by a single thread and left like a bare mannequin in a glass storefront while life mocks me and passes me by.

Three times a day—breakfast, dinner, and bedtime—my husband Marc pops the blister dispenser, 3-2-3 pills each time on the tabletop, and places them in my hand. I swallow the pills with half a glass of warm water. I hate cold things. Afterwards, with the help of my white cane, I move away from the table to the sofa in the living room. As I sit on my couch, I stare into the darkness before me, and I listen to the soft musical notes on a Seattle station that often plays classical music. Andrea Bocelli is singing "Sacred Arias." I doze off when the songs end. Marc is downstairs typing on his computer keyboard.

I don't remember much that has happened to me recently. Like wet snapshots hanging loosely on a string, I remember places in France and Spain: a beach, a castle, a book in my hand, a swarthy young man, and a flight. But I don't remember what the book is about nor the castle I am visiting. I do remember the rustling sound of the pebbles on a beach. Not far from where I am sitting, there is a young man looking at me. Although he pretends not to show it, he persists to look in my direction. I recall driving a Vespa scooter; I recall the same young man riding with me, holding onto my waist. He is a student from Italy. I like his dark, chestnut, wavy hair. He is tall and slender, and I fall in love with him at first sight. I think we marry soon after or we elope—I don't remember which.

His name is Marco. When I introduced Marc to my parents, they didn't like him because he was not French. His family had immigrated to Canada, and I like the idea of travelling to the North American continent. He has a good knowledge of French, and I know he loves to hear my voice with my Midi accent. He loves to read French books and about French history. Did I run away with Marc against my parents' wishes?

In my imagination I am transported to Canada. My first job is teaching French to children in a private school. Then in the evenings I go to school to learn English. In the class I meet many other immigrants, mostly Europeans, among them a French woman who befriends me. Frequently I visit her place in West Bay where she lives. Then things go blank, and I don't remember very much. The French woman has disappeared from my life. Maybe later things will come back to me. Many years have gone by, but right now I am not feeling very well. I have cramps in my stomach, and I think I am going to throw up. I must stop trying to remember.

Marc thinks the medication I am taking doesn't agree with me. We should talk to the doctor again. Our next visit is scheduled too far down the road to be of any good to me. I am sick now. I want this pain to go away now, not next month. I can't sleep and must get up two or three times to go to the bathroom. Marc can't sleep either. Poor Marc, he is the only one who can help me now. At times I feel all choked up and want to scream.

"I want to die! I want to die!" These words fill my aching mind. Nobody cares about me. My friends have deserted me. This is how I feel. And you, my husband, you are losing patience with me. You are too busy spending time on that damn computer of yours writing I don't know what, but I suspect you are writing about me. You cannot fool me! All those questions you ask about me, about my youth and my family. It's nobody's business who I am, what I am, what I think, or what I feel. None of their business!

I tell him off at times. So he knows. But here he is again, this time sitting across from me at the breakfast table and not even hearing the toaster pop up. I have to tell him that my toast is ready. I am waiting for it. I hear scratching on the paper. I think he is writing something on a sheet of paper, his next paragraph perhaps. And then he pops another hot question to me like a toaster pops up burned toast.

"Did you date any other boys before me?"

Why such questions at this time at our age? I can't figure it out. He tells people too much about us, but he doesn't know everything about me, and he is not going to. Why should he? I am my own person, and even after so many years being married to him, he is not entitled to know. People don't always tell you the truth about themselves. They all lie or make up stories. I don't lie and don't make up stories. It's not my nature to tell. It's no one's business to know about someone's private life.

Now people ask what's wrong with me. Before they asked, "How did you become blind?" Now I am asked, "How did you get dementia?" but I remain silent and am afraid to say anything.

After I was tested for memory by the therapist—who asked some silly questions and made me do trick games—I was told that I have Alzheimer's. The physiotherapist asked me questions to which I was supposed to respond yes or no. In one test, I was told to draw the shape of a flag.

"A flag?" A silly question I thought.

"Yes, a flag," said the physiotherapist. "The shape of it."

"French or Canadian? Maybe American?" I asked.

"It doesn't matter," Marc intervened. "It's the same thing, Cosette."

"What thing, Marc?" I asked again.

The physiotherapist patiently suggested that I draw something. "Mrs. Rocca, just draw a rectangle—like a shoebox cover."

Since I don't see, I don't know what the result was, but I could hear Marc scoffing beside me. Sometimes he does that.

"Can you tell me your daughters' birthdates?" The woman asked. That was another silly question, and of course I know my daughters' birthdates. All along, my two daughters had been sitting on either side of me, silent and withdrawn, as if at a funeral parlor arranging my funeral. I began to worry about the questions I was being asked, and I felt awkward. Here was when, I think, I put a hand over my lips and tapped them nervously.

"Birthdays, birthdays, but whose?" I could not put it together. Maybe I was trying to pull out the words from my mouth, but they were imprisoned in my mind.

"Mom? My birthday, two days before Valentine's Day!" Martha nudged me.

"What Valentine? I don't know anyone called Valentine." I could not remember the date. Marc always told me that I had the best memory in the whole family, and now I could not remember an easy date.

"Mom, February. The month is February. You never forgot the day. It's the twelfth of the month." My smart daughter was lecturing me now.

"Okay!" said the therapist, but before she moved down on her list, she popped another question. "Marc's. Do you remember Marc's birthday?"

I would never forget my husband's birthdate. I did not answer. I was embarrassed enough.

The next time I visit Dr. Komo I'll tell him what I think of him. First, there is nothing wrong with me! All the medication he prescribes for me is to make him rich. They make money, all these doctors, with the medications they prescribe for me. Oh, I know, I know. Marc, who's always better informed, tells me, "It's not the doctors who're making money, but the greedy drug companies."

But to me, it's all the same. They all pull the same cart! Sometimes my husband must think I am a bit crazy to talk like that, but that's the way I feel about it. I am entitled to my opinions, aren't I? And sometimes I turn around and wait for Marc's approval.

"Of course, dear, you can say anything you want." He nods his head in a futile gesture.

I am lucky that I have medical coverage from my employer. Often I think that if I didn't have coverage for dental and medical, it would be harder for us from a financial point of view. Marc worked for a private company, but when he retired all his benefits were cut except his small pension, of course. Now he is lucky to be on my plan. And what about our girls? The first born, Charlene, who is almost fifty, is married and with two girls of her own. She has no medical plan and must pay out of her own pocket. Her husband has not fared any better either. Many years ago he quit his government job for a private company, but when the huge American firm bought out the forestry firm he worked for, they downsized and let him go. He is a forester working on his own now, and he has no coverage for his family.

I kept telling my daughters to get good jobs, to work for the government like I did. Fortunately, the second one is a health worker for the government. She and her children have medical and dental coverage, but the children live mostly with their father. Just think about this: her husband, after the divorce, tried to get on her plan as well, the devil. Martha is still entangled in a legal custody battle with her children's father. She is a born loser. She lost a lot of money—most of it ours—fighting her husband in the courts. Worse, she lost two-thirds custody of her children. She is in debt to us and to the banks. I told Marc to stop rescuing her every time she has financial problems.

Looking down the road and if I live long enough, I worry that I may have to go to an assisted living hospice that will cost me and Marc a lot of money. I will need money in the future for a nursing home, a very expensive worry. We may even have to sell our house to pay for my stay. Marc tries to reassure me that there is no need to sell our house, but I always pester him about it.

Sometimes he says, "Cosette, sometimes I think you're nuts and driving me insane also!" I know he doesn't mean that I am crazy, but I don't like when he says that to me. I don't like it one bit.

Yesterday, out of the blue, he asked me, "Did your sister take you along when she went out with her friends? You told me that she liked to fool around with boys."

I don't know what I may or may not have told my husband in the past about my sister, but this time he's really annoying me with his stupid questions. How many times have I told him that I don't want to talk about my sister or my parents? My mother and father are dead and buried, and my sister has her life, as I have mine. Now my sister is dead too— she was no good anyway—and soon I will be dead too if I get my wish! Then the world will leave us all to rest in peace. So leave me alone!

Tomorrow is Thursday, and the regular care worker will come again. She didn't come on Tuesday, because she had a cold. We were told that her co-workers say she gets too many colds.

The agency telephoned. "Would you accept a replacement worker?"

"Yes," I said. "What's her name?"

"Elisabeth."

Elisabeth is from Hong Kong. She is a wonderful worker. I like her. But tomorrow the regular worker comes back. I wish her cold did not go away so that they would send me Elisabeth instead. I like

Elisabeth because she is nice—nicer than the Polish woman. She takes care of me in a very special way. The night I went to bed after she left, I found my pajamas under my pillow and folded neatly. I could feel the care she put into doing it. I told Marc that I liked Elisabeth and that we should try to get her. But he told me not to rush things. He reminded me that Elisabeth was only a replacement for our regular worker. He tried to be nice to me. Told me to wait and see. He promised that if things did not work out with the Polish woman, he would telephone the agency and put in a request for Elisabeth.

This morning Marc had some business to do in the village. From the hall table, he reached for my gloves and my purple beret. From the shoe rack, he selected the black leather boots—the ones with the zipper on the side—and handed them to me. I put them on, and I told Marc that the boots didn't fit. "These damned boots don't fit me anymore."

I think I swore something in Italian, which my husband did not appreciate.

"That's because you are wearing them on the wrong feet!"

From the tone of his voice, I didn't know if it was because I swore or because he thought I put my boots on the wrong way. Anyway, he should have been a bit more tactful.

After he dressed me up with a zippered water-proof anorak, he pulled up an umbrella from the stand by the door and walked to the car. It was sunny, but I could only feel the cold air on my face. I wore gloves because my hands are always freezing. Later Marc drove us to the seniors center for coffee. The center is run mostly by volunteers, and Marc and I are both members. But before lining up for service, Marc checked his pocket for our cards. He found mine but could not find his own. Thinking that he had lost it, he approached the desk to request a new one. The woman took her time at the computer. She was an older lady volunteering her time, Marc told me later, and new technology was not her thing, I suppose. But what was the big rush? We had time.

When the volunteer gave Marc his new card, the woman told him, "Sir, this is the second renewal for you. The last one was dated December 19, 2012. Remember, next time you have to pay a renewal fee."

After that we went to the Garden Café for coffee and pastry. You need to have a membership card to get a discount when dining there. To get your senior's discount, you must first place your member-ship cards on the tray with the food you select and pay for the meal with cash or with a credit card. The cashier runs your amount on the machine and tells you what you owe. Many people nowadays pay with credit cards. When it was my husband's turn to pay, he pulled his VISA from his wallet, and that's when the card he thought he had lost dropped to the floor.

I didn't see this, but I heard the cashier tell my husband, "Sir, you dropped the other card. Is it yours also?"

"No, no. It's my daughter's," he replied.

I know he lied. Poor Marc. I think he is losing it too. Later he told me the card was stuck in with his credit card. When we sat down at a table near the garden entrance of the café, I heard many voices and the sound of cups and cutlery. When we had finished with our coffee and muffins, I heard a shuffling sound across from me—someone approaching. I smelled a woman's perfume as she commented on the sweater I was wearing.

"What a beautiful design. I like the colors and the texture. You have good taste." Then she walked away.

Yes, I told myself, I *had* good taste, but not anymore. I don't know if what she said was true or if she said something nice to me because she saw that I am blind (I had my white cane with me). But then again, good taste for clothing goes with good eyesight. When we walked to our car outside, I asked Marc if the woman really meant to congratulate me for the sweater.

He said, "The woman is from my bowling club. I know she meant what she said." And then, also complimenting me, he added, "Yes, dear, that really is a nice sweater you have. It's the black one with a fish scale design and checkered diamond shapes of black and purple. You have always had good taste when buying items of clothing for yourself."

*   *   *

I was resting alone in the living room upstairs and needed to go to the washroom badly. The radio was on. I called out for Marc. I thought he was again at his computer in the study. He did not hear me at first. I tapped my cane on the wall once, and not hearing my husband's response, I began to worry.

Was he out? Was he in the wine cellar downstairs at the back of the house checking his latest wine purchases? I needed to go badly. I tapped my cane hard on the floor one more time. He heard the tapping, and I waited. I know he is hard of hearing and does not always wear his hearing aids; he complains his ears sweat too much.

"What's up, dear? Do you need anything?" my husband asked in an offhand way.

Of course I needed him. I had been calling and calling! Did he want me to pee in my panties? He wanted me to wear pads.

"Where are you?" I yelled.

Then I heard him racing up the steps, two at a time. "*O! Merde,*" he swore in French. I think he forgot the rope strung at the top of the staircase to keep me safe. I think he paused to take a breather and compose himself before he got to me and guided me hastily into the bathroom. I felt pee trickling down my legs just as I lifted the lid and undid my panties to sit on the toilet. That's what you get when you are late helping me, you fool! I thought.

"It's OK, it's OK. Dear, I'm sorry!" He kept apologizing. And then he went on. "Don't worry. It's not a big deal! I will help you shower and change you afterwards. I'll clean up the mess."

Marc sometimes gets frustrated with me when I wake him up to go to the washroom in the dead of night. He gets impatient when his sleep gets disturbed. Nights are especially difficult for me, and that's when I really need to go. Usually my husband is very good at caring for me, but the other night when I asked him to take me to the bathroom, he complained. "You know the way: follow along the bed, turn right, then left, and again right. The toilet is on the right. Don't forget to lift up the lid first."

I panicked. I don't know what is left and what is right anymore. He knows I get confused when I am alone and need to go. I always need help now! Finally he woke up and, jumping from the bed, he rushed to help me. I guess he had fallen asleep after a night of tossing and turning. With difficulty, I returned to my bed without his help, but I had trouble falling asleep. I soon began sobbing. Clenching my teeth, I tried not to cry. But cried out of despair and loneliness. I felt so down I wished I were dead. Then an angel came to my rescue. I felt a warm hand, soft as a wing, searching my face. It was searching for the cause of my sobbing.

Marc woke up. He felt guilty—how could he have slept through that and not been aware of it sooner? Tenderly he kissed my hand that I had placed across my face to hide my shame. He moved closer, took me, and held me in his arms. When I was close to him I touched his face; it was wet. His tears joined mine on the soft pillow of down feathers.

The week after, he went out and bought me a commode that he placed beside my bed. "So that you don't have to walk to the bathroom," he said.

However, this has only worked temporarily. I have had difficulty opening and closing the lid to seal the smell of urine, and so I have kept waking Marc during the night to help me. Marc is resigned to his duty. What choice does he have?

*　　　*　　　*

February 14, 2013—Valentine's day. I slept in, but I felt Marc's wet lips kissing my forehead and his hand caress my face. "Time to wake up. Happy Valentine's, dear!"

The word Valentine triggered the switch in my brain. Was it someone's name? Or was it a place? Was it somebody's birthday?

He kissed me again on my dry lips.

"What's Valentine's, Marc?"

"It's a time to be kind to the one you're in love with."

Why? Who are you in love with, Marc?

"No matter, dear. It's a nice day, a special day. You are special." So my husband tells me, then goes on to more important topics. "Breakfast is ready—your favorite: coffee, yogurt mixed with cereal and topped with sliced bananas."

He fetches the medication blisters and pops my pills.

Breakfast. Every morning is printed in bold letters on the label above the blisters.

"But before you start eating, this is what I say: here are your pills. Pills and kisses make ills go away." He tries to amuse me. Then he asks, "Now, open your hand."

I open my left hand. He places the tablets in my palm and hands me a glass of warm water to swallow with the pills in my right hand. His own hands have been quite full lately, but also ready to serve.

"Here is the first installment for the day for your elixir of life!" More funny sayings to cheer me up.

It was a sunny and cold morning, Marc said. The layer of frost on the flat roof of the school across the street had vanished, evaporated, as he described it, in a gentle steam rising high in the still-frosty air. Recalling our girls, Marc said that school children were streaming down the sidewalk across from our home on their way to classes. I detected a quiver in his voice. Led by their mothers, the small ones were all bundled up in warm clothing, and older kids walked to school by themselves, some sauntering happily.

"Do you remember when our girls went to school there? All they had to do was walk to the bottom of the driveway, wait, look left, right, and left again, then cross to the other side, and they were at the school entrance. Then back home for lunch every day. They always came home for lunch break. They sure had it easy, our girls!"

I had a feeling of joy when Marc mentioned the girls going to primary school right in front of our house. I guess I am not the vivacious young mother of many years ago. I had energy then to do all the things I did for them. Often I worked nights to help Marc out with our family finances. But my husband complained that most of what I earned I spent for the girls' activities, rushing them from one class to another during the weekends and on my days off. Yes, it's true I wanted my girls to have the best of everything: ballet, music, gymnastics, skating, swimming, you name it. I really stretched myself thin though. Marc said that maybe all this driving around non-stop had affected my health. He had often warned me about it.

"Don't do so much—you'll pay the price one day."

Did I do too much? Does a mother do too much for her children? I know I never got enough rest for myself. Now that I am slow, can't think straight, and don't remember much, I blame myself for it.

Because I walk slowly, a friend told me I might have *gait*. I didn't know what the word meant. I'd never heard it before. I asked Marc. He said he was not familiar with the word, so he looked it up in *Webster's Dictionary*. He told me it means *a manner of walking, of moving the feet.*

I learn something every day now: new behavior, new words, new definitions. It's strange though. One has to be an invalid to learn new things. Life is putting me through the mill once more. I guess I have a bulb on my head that switches on and off at will, but I have no control over the pull switch.

To let fresh air in, the attending care person has left the sundeck door partly open. I can feel where the morning sun has warmed up the sundeck. The woman was making my bed with clean, fresh-smelling sheets. She will then take the dirty ones downstairs to the laundry room.

"Staying cooped up inside most of the day is not good for you," Marc has said.

My husband insists that I get plenty of fresh air, but I don't like it when he refers to me as a caged bird that needs to be freed from enslavement by the care worker. But of course he doesn't mean anything bad in saying that.

"It's only a matter of speaking," he says. "We just want to take good care of you." he repeats. He decides to walk me to the sundeck. He pulls out a chair and asks me to sit, but I have difficulty with the plastic chair. It's not comfortable enough.

"Move your back away from the back of the chair so I can slide the cushion behind you for more comfort," Marc counsels me.

But I remain sitting askew at the edge of the chair, uncertain as to what to do. Back away... the back of the chair ... behind you—all of this confuses me. Something in my mind lights up. Words and images swirl in, and something comes slowly into focus. The past talks to me, but it is a cacophony of chatter, like pebbles rubbed together by eddies in the ebb of my life. The light bulb goes out again, and the picture is blurred.

*   *   *

Late September, 1975. Strange, I remember the year because it was Marc's 40th . Last week we moved into our new home (not exactly new—it was built in 1954 by Lewis Contractors, a low-budget builder of the time specializing in post-and-beam structures). When looking for a home to buy, we stopped at an open sign at a house for sale on Mathers Avenue in the Ambleside area. The owner of the house was an "architect" (a draftsman in fact), who had an office on the lower floor. Marc too worked as a draftsman at the time and could make use of the drafting table left behind.

When we visited the house, we noted it was rundown and not quite appealing, but the location was ideal. With southerly views of the harbor, Stanley Park, and the Lions Gate Bridge, it could be a steal Marc said. The house needed repairs, however, and upgrading to more modern standards was a must.

Fittingly, Marc saw great potential in the house, and the girls too showed strong interest in it as well. It was close to a school, had a pool and a great backyard. I disliked it because it was old, but then I had forgotten that Marc had the knack of a good handyman. Later he would transform it into a pleasant, modern home with happy days ahead. On the contrary, my eyes were set on a modern, Japanese-style structure that would be located higher up the hill and offer higher affordability for West Coast living. Nonetheless, the three of them ganged up on me.

Marc made an offer on the low side and thought it didn't stand a change of being accepted. We then went home and took the girls for an outing to the park. When we returned home the phone rang; it was the real estate agent.

"Mr. Rocca, I am pleased to inform you that the offer has been accepted. We need to see you and your wife to complete the transaction."

We were having dinner. I choked. When I looked at Marc, he must have seen tears forming in my eyes. The offer was accepted, and I was terribly disappointed. We got the house, and here I am now still enjoying this old house that I did not want to own because of my selfishness. This house has been where my dreams were made. It is where I have been so happy despite the adversity of my handicap. It has been so convenient and close to a school for my children, and it is close to a bus route that came in handy for me when I went to work.

I hear school bells ring at recess. I hear happy, squealing voices storming out of the classrooms into the playgrounds. From the sundeck I spot my two neatly dressed girls coming up the trail, then walking up the driveway to the house.

Noting me by the railing on the sundeck, Charlene greets me with her young, happy voice.

"Hello Maman, is lunch ready? We are hungry!" Charlene greets.

Anticipating her meal, I hear little Martha smacking her lips like a puppy. "*Je voudrais* peanut butter sandwich and carrot sticks," she says in French-English and rushes ahead to the door.

"And for me, I want French toast, the special way you make. C'*est delicieux!*" When at the door, Charlene addresses her sister. "*Attend, Martha*, I have the key."

Since we moved to the North Shore, it has always been half-French half-English. Soon it will be English only. They are the only two French-speaking girls in class, and they wear earrings in school. They are a bit of an oddity with a French mother and Italian father with the last name Rocca. They tell me the other children tease them because of their funny looks and funny accents. Two other girls, also with Italian last names, once attended school, but they moved away long ago.

I hear my two girls climb up the stairs and rush to the dining room, where their meal is waiting at the table. Now here they are, my two jewels brightening up the house, making me happy. *Les deux bijoux,* their French grandmere called them.

My girls are grown-ups now and have their own jewels (two in particular, Bella and Stella—Sharlene's girls). Martha's children—Elena, Nunzia, and the boy, Sam—have been snatched from their mother's love by an uncaring father who continues to alienate them from us. For this, my heart bleeds.

But for now I am contemplating the forty years spent in this house where my dreams were made, and the almost sixty years ago that I left my parents in France. It has flown by on the wings of time. And like a river, with twists and bends, life itself has flown down its channel that has seen calm and, at times, turbulence. What I try to retain in the view-finder of my mind are now only felt in the changes of each season with its smells and perfumes but not its visual glory and beauty that I cannot see. With my hands, I felt Marc's aging face. I have touched the furrowed folds of his forehead, I tasted his tears with my lips, and I wept in my heart. I miss seeing my granddaughters growing in the spring of their lives, but I still remember the youngest telling me once, "Grandma, I am so sorry, for you cannot see me growing up."

Slowly their faces have vanished, but the longing for their presence is an ache in my heart.

Now I miss many things in my life. It's a litany of complaints, or is it my funeral? I miss driving my own car, but then I lost that when I became blind. I miss doing the laundry, doing the ironing. I miss showering by myself and dressing myself, choosing my own clothes to wear and where to go buy them without someone's assistance. I miss even the small things, like buying lipstick or a pair of stockings. I can't eat properly using a fork or a spoon. Now I use my hands to put food in my mouth, and when I am taken out where there are other people around, I know they are watching me. I miss all the things that a normal, independent woman would do, pure and simple.

I guess I am not "normal" anymore. My life is cut in half, and I am reduced to asking for help when eating, walking, turning on the radio, calling a friend on the telephone, or even going pee on my own. I have all my limbs, but they don't work either often not responding to command. I am slow, terribly slow when I walk, when I try to get into bed, when I eat, and even when I talk. I am so miserable. I was given the name Cosette. My parents wanted me to be nothing and miserable by naming me Cosette: the little thing. My name has been a curse for me!

I remember a letter I wrote to my parents. Marc found it in a drawer in the house in France before we sold it. Marc said he had never seen it, as it was addressed to my parents. One day he read it to me.

This is what I wrote.

West Vancouver, BC, September 12, 1977

> *Dear parents,*
>
> *The days and nights go by, and I am always putting things off until next*

time. But I can tell you that this year we have had a wonderful summer—only during one week we had some rain. Do you remember? You should have come to visit us this year!

Besides that, all is going for the better: our jobs, the garden, the house, the children—all of that keeps us busy. I must tell you though that this summer we had pool parties every Saturday and Sunday, and, sometimes even during the week, which was a bit too much. I told Marc and the girls to put a stop to that. But as you know, Marc and the children love to have friends and enjoy the pool. We have invited friends and family since May of this year until September. Now it's time to be invited back.

Some people are very envious of us because we live in a big house with a swimming pool in West Vancouver. I have bought myself a new set of bedding furniture, for which I paid dearly. Also, this year we had to replace the pool filter and the motor. All of this has cost us dearly. In addition, the tenants we had in the old house have moved out without paying the rent. It has been left vacant for the last three months. We had to buy a new fridge, because the tenants broke the old one. Needless to say, this year we did not save any money.

Oh yes, we have changed to the Metric system, just like in France. The children have returned to class. Charlene is in grade seven, Martha is in grade five. We hope to make something out of our two girls. It's worth saying that Charlene took first prize in French language, with a book from the French Consulate. Soon we hope she will send you a long letter written in French. On the twelfth of February she will have her confirmation. For this we have invited many relatives and friends. At the end of the fall this year, we also celebrated Marc's parents 50th anniversary. We had sixty people in our house. After that I said no more big parties and told Marc I wished to visit Italy and spend some money travelling instead.

Besides that, everything else is all right. My work at the hospital revolves around two week days, two week nights.

Truly I wish to switch to the maternity ward, as presently I am working in the geriatric department, where I see too much suffering, and some of the patients aren't always nice. It's too depressing. It is now five years that I am working in this ward of the hospital, and I need a change.

In closing, the girls have resumed their lessons in ballet, swimming, and skating. So everyday I am a taxi driver. I truly hope that one day the two demoiselles will be grateful for everything their mother is doing for them.

Love,
Cosette

*   *   *

It's Sunday afternoon. To challenge myself, I ask Marc to take me out for a stroll in the park. But I warned him not to expect me to trot much but to go slowly. After all, I am not a horse but just a slow-walking invalid. Marc chuckles at my remark. He is not going to ride me, he says, but just lead me. He's only a faceless caregiver now, he tells me.

I feel I have not always appreciated what Marc has done for me, and I am sorry for it. But now sometimes I live in another world, an insidious world of evil spirits that move in unannounced, especially at night when I need my rest, and bring with them their terrible moments of self-destruction. But I have the right to know my full life before I renounce it. Something alien enters my mind and drives me almost insane. I become another person sometimes, mean-spirited and short-fused. Is this the reason I want to die? But why? What force inhabits the recesses of my mind that I must wish myself dead? Ho! How sorry I am for Marc to have to witness this.

CHAPTER 14

March 7, 2013 was the day after the storm. Last night I feared I was going to lose my wife.

It was a long, painful, and dreaded night. Unknown to me at the time as the evening advanced into night, Cosette had been alone in the bathroom brushing her teeth. There she had mistaken a bottle of nail polish remover, carelessly left on the bathroom counter, for mouthwash. I suspect she swallowed some of the harmful liquid along with some baby aspirin. It was the night her mind exited her body, leaving a trail of almost total disconnection in its wake. I truly felt Cosette's mind was snatched from her, and that feeling was the most heart-wrenching.

Was this the time when the eternal darkness would swallow her? Was there something I did wrong to deserve this calamitous tragedy? Did I not foresee incidents like these happening? Surely it was a moment when blood rushed to my brain and froze. All of this had come at a time when, only the day before, I had paid for our trip to France, a trip she so badly wanted to take, and on the eve of hiring a new care worker. All these events combined may have triggered the outburst that came next.

Surfacing unexpectedly, tenseness and then agitation appeared on our way to the bedroom upstairs. She was having difficulty changing into her pajamas. She hesitated, picked up a pillow from the bed, and began smacking it repeatedly with force. Then she cried out, "This is not my bed; this is not my home. I want to go home, I want to go home and die."

I approached her and held her tightly in my arms. I kissed her hot forehead, hoping she would settle down.

"Let me be! You are suffocating me," she shouted.

She finally entered the bed. But it was not long before she would start whimpering. Her mood swung to uncontrollable bouts of shaking, almost convulsive.

"My bed, I wet my bed!" she cried out, hallucinating.

I pulled myself out of the bed and ran to her side. Dreading the worst, I uncovered the sheets, almost stripping the whole bed apart. There was no sign of wetness in the bed, but I tried to get her up and guide her to the bathroom. Her body was stiff in my arms; I placed her on the toilet.

"No, no!" she protested.

I had to help her to pee; she could not do it alone. But she resisted me. Holding her fast in front of me, I lowered her pajamas and then her panties. I heard a rush of urine spouting out into the bowl. I helped her back to our bed, pulled the covers over her convulsing body, and returned to my side of the bed.

She had forgotten how to get up and ask to be guided to the washroom. She needed to relieve herself, but her mind could not interpret it rightly. Her body was no longer a function of her brain. Her faulty brain sent out faulty messages for her to function properly. She was in the realm of irrational and magical thinking. The wires were disconnected, and I was not capable of putting them back together, nor were doctors able to look into their crystal balls to discover why the wires weren't connected properly. For this they had to look into her brain, which was out of sync with her body.

That was the night Cosette melted, sucked into a dark vortex.

I died with her.

I may have miscalculated my plans to take my wife traveling to France to visit her relatives. I may have also badly miscalculated the plans to add a cruise from Venice to Balcelona. It would have entailed travelling by train from Paris to Narbonne in southern France, and then from Narbonne to Venice for the Mediterranean cruise to Barcelona. Finding accommodations in Venice was expensive, but traveling with a blind wife with dementia would be daunting. When my daughter Charlene came to visit us with the children for spring break, she reproved me regarding this very matter.

"Dad, are you sure you want to take Mother on such a long trip, knowing full well that Mom is not well?"

*   *   *

April 22, 2013. Today was the day we were supposed to board a flight for Paris. A certain amount of careful planning had taken place prior to this day. Despite our daughter's rebuke, it was supposed to be a joyous departure for Cosette to reunite with her relatives in France, especially her elderly aunt Alice who would be ninety-three-years old that year. Her cousins, who lived in the periphery of Paris, also looked ahead to seeing her again. But dark clouds had begun to gather even before our plans had been made to include a cruise voyage from Venice to Barcelona. Three weeks earlier I had made plans to bus downtown with Cosette to purchase a new pair of slacks for myself. Recommended to me by a friend from the bowling club, the store Madison was located at the corner of Thurlow and Pender Streets in downtown Vancouver. On the way back Cosette felt sick, and the chronic fainter did it again.

She needed to take a rest, but she quickly slumped on my shoulder. I panicked. I asked for help. Fearing that she would pass out before we made it to the bus stop on Georgia Street, a passer-by called a cab for us. The cab took us to our parked car in South Park Royal in West Vancouver. From there, we transferred to my car and left for home.

For now the wild horses of Camargue and the explosion of lavender in the fields of Provence had to wait for the war waging in Cosette mind's to abate. In the meantime, I needed to stop taking my cancer medication and keep some modest libido in my life. But that decision could come back to haunt me, especially after I read an editorial in the *Vancouver Sun* newspaper implying that "The sword of Damocles could hang over my head" much sooner. In reading the article, I was reassured at least in the short run about my chances and consoled myself about the prospect that I would probably live long enough to continue caring for my wife. The column is reprinted here in part with the *Vancouver Sun*'s permission. (9)

> *Increasingly common prostate cancer will hit one in two men.*
>
> The good news? Screening is catching it earlier and the mortality rate declining
>
> Imagine this. Through no fault of your own, you were born with a chromosome that makes you highly susceptible to developing a potentially fatal disease.
>
> In fact, one in seven people with your genetic makeup will develop the disease at some point in their lives, and one in 28 will die from it. And unlike genetic conditions such as Down syndrome, this isn't something you're born with - rather, your risk of developing the disease increases dramatically as you age.
>
> Even worse, unlike many diseases, the incidence of this disease has increased over the last 30 years. And while living a healthy lifestyle can probably help

to reduce your chances of becoming one of those unlucky souls, there is no known single cause of the disease. So thanks to your genetics, you are simply condemned to living your life with this sword of Damocles hanging over your head.

And worst of all, the odds of you being a member of this unfortunate group is one in two—because the group is the male sex and the disease is prostate cancer....

But the sad news is that prostate cancer still takes the lives of many men.

*   *   *

Incontinence was her new blemish. A new railing was installed upstairs along the corridors, and a new one for the stairs going up to the second floor. This was done to facilitate Cosette walking to and from the two floors of the house, but also to aid her in locating the bedroom and main bathroom upstairs.

"I have to go now. Guide me to the toilet," she announced from the living room, where she sat on a sofa. This call repeated itself over and over many times.

"Rise up from where you are sitting, turn left, go to the wall, take the railing, and go to the bathroom."

Despite my good intentions, my words were met with another cry for help.

"This is the fourth time you've called in the last hour. In all, it's been a dozen time since you got up." Greatly annoyed, I protested.

"No, this is the first," she responded. "You lie to me—you have no patience," she continued.

"Stop arguing with me. "You are wearing disposable diapers. Go ahead, use them." "I don't *want* to wet them," she said, embarrassed.

"That's what they are for. You can relieve yourself any time."

"But I don't want you to wash them."

"I don't have to wash them. I throw them in the trash bin."

"But people will know I use them."

"Nobody will know."

"Yes they will. People snoop."

"Fuck the people. I don't care what people might say."

"I'm going to jump off a bridge! That's what I am going to do," she snarled back.

"Then go piss off!" I shouted back, angered. I was shocked at my rudeness. But I couldn't go on like this. I didn't have time to do anything else, especially working on my computer downstairs. It was a constant going up and down for her nagging cries for help. I knew I should not act in such an annoyed, uncouth way. But I was beginning to feel the exhaustion piling up.

While shopping at Safeway yesterday, I left Cosette in the car for about fifteen minutes. When I came out of the store, I noted a great commotion around my car. People were milling around, curious and fretting. I panicked, nearly dropping my shopping bags as I approached. I dreaded what might have happened. Assuming I wasn't coming back, Cosette panicked. She sounded the horn in distress. Onlookers rushed in. Agitated, she had lodged herself between the seat and the front panel of the dashboard.

The next evening, while I left her in the family room watching TV, she panicked again, remembering the night before.

"You left me. I didn't know where I was," she sobbed helplessly.

She wanted to go to bed early. In the bedroom I undressed her, helped her with her pajamas, opened the covers, and tucked her in.

"Don't forget the commode. I need it close to my bed. Is the lid up or down?" she asked.

The other night, as I slept, Cosette tried to use the commode all by herself. In doing so, she lost her balance and fell, hitting the nightstand. This resulted in a broken rib on her left side. She cried herself back to sleep. When I checked on her in the morning, she had quite a number of bruises on her body. When I took her to the doctor the next day, he confirmed the broken rib but offered no remedy, as there was little he could do for a broken rib.

"Give her some Tylenol to ease the pain, and make sure she gets lots of rest," he advised.

Poor Cosette, one indignity after another. Life sometimes sure picked on the most unfortunate and defenseless.

Daily and nightly, these incidents and occurrences would repeat with regularity. Unable to do many things on her own, I inevitably had to be proactive. I was required to help and provide for her night and day, no matter what. She needed help constantly, and I was there to give it to her. But I had to stop whining to myself, or this would lead me to incapacity.

*   *   *

Spring is in the air. I am up early, and I make myself a cup of coffee with my favorite blend of Hawaiian and Costa Rican beans. With the cup in hand, I move to the kitchen window that looks out to the backyard. Patches of blue sky had begun appearing from the west. Cosette was still sleeping. To celebrate some unnamed occasion, last night we foolishly indulged in some bubbly. We even dispensed with all the pills she was supposed to take for one evening. She needed lots of sleep these days. Tomorrow the cleaning woman would come to put order to our home that had suffered from lack of good housekeeping since Cosette's onset of dementia. Ruby would vacuum the carpets and wash the kitchen floor. She would clean and put away all dishes and pots and pans used in last night's dinner (I used too many pots when I cooked). She would also make our bed after Cosette was up. All house chores I could not do alone anymore.

Through the window I could see the flocks of finches landing gracefully on our backyard garden. They brought new life after the dead of winter. For a long moment, my mind took flight to a distant land of my birthplace, far away high on the Abruzzo hills. But it was not new life that birds brought to me then but death by a trap. It was winter. Sparrows landed on the snow in front of our stone house, in front of which I had set traps to catch them. The little sparrows made meager morsels on the *polenta* at our table, but better than going hungry. Nearly sixty years had gone by since I left a land no longer mine. I recalled the skinny boy climbing up to a distant rocky, treeless ridge. The wind was blowing in his face, ruffling his thick black hair. From the hills and sweeping away down to the valley below, he perceived the river of his life flowing in twists and bends. He would go to school, study, and then forsake his land. But the river returned, obstinate. It still existed, but it flowed in the wrong direction in a land not under his feet but in the crevices of his mind. Then another image appeared of my dear mother sitting under the rhododendron tree. Only her back was visible, silhouetted against the blue of the swimming pool in the backyard. Always wise, always inspiring and compromising, she left me with a commandment, and her words of wisdom still rang in my ears.

"My son, no matter what, you must take care of your wife Cosette. She will need you for years to come."

When I had a few moments alone during my respite, and I was with friends, I looked for a word of encouragement, a hand on my shoulder to carry on my role of caregiver. I needed this to continue to take care for Cosette.

Was there life remaining? This beautiful human life that was Cosette? Would I still be there to care for her?

I remembered the time. I remembered the place. I remembered the beach in France, the fig trees in

Spain. And, like a pebble in my shoe, I remembered the sacred soil we once walked on and the vow of "rich and poor, in health and sickness," and I could not let go. I remembered Cosette alive and well.

*　　　*　　　*

June 25, 2013, a visit to our doctor that remained etched in my soul.

The weeks before, Cosette had developed swollen legs. She could hardly walk without feeling much pain. The doctor had prescribed some medication that was supposed to reduce the swelling, but this never happened. What happened is that Dr. Smith instructed me to take Cosette to emergency at Lions Gate Hospital immediately. Again, as before, Cosette went through the routine of checks and tests of her health status. By the next morning, I was told she had suffered congenitive heart failure, a kidney and bladder infection, and she would require immediate cardiac and renal attention if she were to survive. The doctors and nurses worked feverishly to save her life. Now I knew she would not come back home.

She was still at Lions Gate Hospital when, without being told, she was transferred to another ward. It was a waiting ward in general medicine, a sort of catching pool for future transfers to other facilities outside the hospital. Unfortunately, the level of care was not adequate. I visited her three times a day, and while I waited it out, she waited for me so I could wait on her—that is how depended she was on me.

The week after her stay in general medicine, Cosette was transferred again, this time to a care home next to the hospital: Evergreen House. Her condition deteriorated rapidly. Unexpectedly, her moods became more prone to swinging, and these changes were often difficult to handle. As she was now shut off from outside activities, her spiritual needs were not fulfilled, as we had not attended church for the last six weeks. Only one visit from a visiting priest, and that was for the assumed last unction. Unexpectedly, the tzunami hit. She was wheeled into emergency again.

Two hours later she was gone.

I would be pacing the very floors she walked on, touching the very same walls she touched as she shuffled about, tapping away with her white cane. Her voice would not resonate and be joy to my ears. I would be alone in a lonely, empty house.

*   *   *   *

Cosette was dreaming. Her mom was calling her—a voice from whence she came.

"Cosette, it's me, *ta Maman*. Aren't you coming to church? Mass starts at ten."

She could see and hear angels singing; they sang in Latin.

KYRIE eleison,

kyrie eleison,

Christe eleison

She saw a woman in a halo of bright light walking to the altar to receive the host. A choir was singing.

Attende Domine et miserere,

Qui a peccavimus tibi.

Attende.

Hear us, O Lord, and have mercy / Because we have sinned against Thee. Hear us.

She got up from bed, put on her white robe, and wandered into the hallway, childlike.

She murmured one word repeated. *Maman, Maman.* She pleaded, lost in the still, dark surroundings. But there was an ethereal grace in the way she moved toward the light at the end of the hallway. Finally, from darkness she entered the eternal light.

"Farewell, farewell, Marc. Until we meet again." And she was gone.

*　　*　　*

Today I was in church alone. It was the second Sunday of Lent. It was a special religious day, but I was unshaven and unkempt. The parish was hosting the Redeemer Pacific Chamber Choir to sing at today's mass. Assembled in a crescent upstairs, in the church loft, members of the choir prepared to sing cappella Gregorian hymns. When they sang "Our Father," Cosette was not beside me holding my hand as usual. When I looked around, the church was full, but the space beside me was empty. It was not a somber service, but a joyous moment burst out when the choir intoned the Ave Regina. The music was soft at first, a beautiful blend of voices singing heartfelt praises, then became a crescendo with the energy of the soul and the heart that cannot be controlled but needs to be acted upon. I searched for the hand that wasn't there. There was a swell of emotion and a lump in my throat choking me, tears blurring my eyes. When it was time to receive communion, I didn't wait for my turn to line up but exited the pew with clenched teeth, my right hand pressed on my left breast. I moved ahead with wary steps.

"Should I take communion? Am I worthy of it?" I asked, confused.

Many parishioners had already lined up in front of me. As I drew nearer the priest, who wore purple vestments (Ferial) and stood before the altar, I opened my right palm to receive Him. When I walked back to my pew, I felt comforted, and I sat down. I felt the gentle tap of an angel's hand on my shoulder.

"I will pray for your wife," said the parishioner sitting behind me, her hand almost clutching me.

Overwhelmed, I turned around to thank her just as I was met by a blast of morning sun filtered through a stained glass window depicting the Last Supper. The light glowed on her blond hair and smiling face.

Later, when I returned home, the house was filled with emptiness. Once there I cried but tried not to drown in the river of grief that ran in my heart. Now it was the sweet memory of the times spent together that kept me afloat.

END

PERMISSIONS AND ACKNOWLEDGMENTS

(1) Puigcerdà was unique during the Spanish Civil War in having a democratically elected anarchist council. Franco's planes laid ruin to the town.

(2) Avieno, Rufo Festo (2001). *Fenomenos* Editorial Gredos, Madrid. Latin poet of the IV Century..

(3) Morella, Editorial Escudo De Oro, S.A.—Barcelona.

(4) Patient.co.uk. Trusted medical information and support.

(5) Prostate Cancer Canada Dr. G. Bristow, contribution to the production of the booklet.

(6) "The intelligent patient guide to Prostate Cancer", by S. Larry Goldberg, MD and Ian M.Thompson, MD.

(7) *The Age of Reason* by J.P. Sartre, Penguin Books, reprinted in 1962, printed in Great Britain by C.Nichols and Company Ltd.

(8) "Just Diagnosed. A guide for men and loved ones."

(9) *Vancouver Sun* editorial—with kind permission (Sandra Boutilier- Librarian)

(10) *Writing Our Way Home*, Licia Canton and Caroline Di Giovanni, Editors. Guernica Editions.

(11) The Group of Seven*, from Mc Michael Canadian Art Collection.

(*) "In the early decades of the twentieth century, circumstances brought together several artists who were committed to exploring, through art, the unique character of the Canadian landscape. The seven artists were: Lawrence Harris, J.E.H,

MacDonald, Arthur Lismer, Frederick Varley, Frank Johnston, Franklin Carmichael, and A.Y. Jackson.

(12) Our amazing brain: Ways to Enhance Learning & Memory, by Becky Brechin, R.N. BScN.

(13) Congestive Heart Failure (CFH). Had been previously detected on October 2012, but not confirmed by the cardiologist.

(14) From Lifescript. Healthy Living For Women.

WORDS OF ENDORSEMENT:

A person who can write... a manuscript on a subject so profound and personal as detailed in Cosette, is deserving of much credit and admiration...

Ray Culos, writer. Burnaby, BC

I think that this story is the real story here and it
is a love story, and one worth telling. The story is a
compelling one and … a good one.

Elspeth Richmond—Editor, Bookmark Editing
and Indexing. North Vancouver, BC

*Io credo che hai fatto una cosa molto coraggiosa a divi-
dere queste tue esperienze… e'un grosso valore dividere
le esperienze in modo cosi chiaro e lineare …*

I believe you have undertaken a courageous path
in writing about these experiences…it has a great
value sharing them in a way so clear and linear…

Anna Foschi Ciampolini—Writer-journalist. North
Vancouver, BC

Bravo!

Bernice Lever—Poet, Writer, and Editor. Bowen
Island, BC.

Printed in Canada